# PARADISE ISLAND

## Hilary Wilde

**CHIVERS**

**THORNDIKE**

This Large Print book is published by BBC Audiobooks Ltd, Bath, England and by Thorndike Press®, Waterville, Maine, USA.

Published in 2005 in the U.K. by arrangement with the author
Published in 2005 in the U.S. by arrangement with Juliet Burton Literary Agency

U.K. Hardcover  ISBN 1–4056–3158–9  (Chivers Large Print)
U.K. Softcover  ISBN 1–4056–3159–7  (Camden Large Print)
U.S.  Softcover  ISBN 0–7862–7021–7  (Nightingale)

The text of this Large Print edition is unabridged.
Other aspects of the book may vary from the original edition.

Set in 16 pt. New Times Roman.

Printed in Great Britain on acid-free paper.

**British Library Cataloguing in Publication Data available**

**Library of Congress Control Number: 2004111182**

# PARADISE ISLAND

# CHAPTER ONE

As the plane circled high above the small island far below them in the blue sea, Lauren Roubin thought it looked like a green jewel. Was that their destination? She stared at it eagerly. This was like a dream come true. She had three months of bliss ahead of her—three months of enjoyable work and long leisurely hours basking in the sunshine on this island off the African coast, instead of shivering in an English winter.

'Fasten your safety belts, please.' The crisp voice shattered the laughter and chatter in the plane, stilling it momentarily. Obediently Lauren's hands found the safety belt.

She was a slight, very pretty girl, elegantly and expensively dressed. She looked rather like a model with her ash-blonde hair lacquered into an elaborate hair-style and crowned by an absurd hat of blue feathers, her high cheekbones made prominent by the discreet use of rouge; her eyes, shadowed lightly, had dark curling lashes and were a cool grey; her mouth was a challenging crimson, and yet, with it all, she gave an impression of shyness and lacked the finished poise of a model.

'Day-dreaming as usual, honey child?' the man by her side said teasingly. He was tall,

1

lean, with a humorous face and dark smooth hair, and his smile at Lauren was friendly. 'Who were you dreaming about?'

Her cheeks hot, her eyes avoided his. If only she could find a way to stop herself from blushing! 'No one,' she said airily, and hoped he would believe her. How could she admit the truth? And confess that she was dreaming about Roland Harvey, the world-famous explorer?

How Nick would laugh and tell her it was time she grew out of teenage crushes! But it was not a crush. She would never forget the day she had first seen him. It had been cold and wet and foggy, and one of the girls from the hostel had taken her to a lecture in a dreary Bayswater hall. Lauren had been reluctant to go, but the instant the tall, impressive-looking man had walked on to the platform, her whole life had seemed to change.

Roland Harvey was a man in his mid-thirties—tall, with rugged good looks and smooth dark red hair. He was world-famous for climbing mountains, and exploring jungles and deserts. He was always doing the impossible with apparent ease.

Roland Harvey had told them about his adventures down the Amazon, and Lauren could almost smell the damp humid atmosphere, hear the chattering of the monkeys and the loud cries of the parrots; he talked of the mountains of the Himalayas, and she had seen those vast slopes, the terrific heights, sheer drops and the enigmatic men as he described them. She had not needed the beautiful coloured slides to make them come to life, for his deep, vibrant voice, his easy command of words had done that for her, but it was the man himself who had made the deepest impression of all.

Tall, broad-shouldered, Roland Harvey had a tough leanness that spelled physical fitness. His voice was full of authority. Here was a man, she felt, who knew what he wanted and would get it. She had sensed the hidden depths in him; the quick temper, the impatience with fools, the strong will, the ruthlessness—but it was all, she had felt strongly, disciplined.

Disciplined. That was the perfect word to describe him. It made him not only fascinating to watch, to listen to—but it made him disturbing, perhaps a little frightening.

The night after the lecture she had dreamed about him. The next day she had gone to the library and asked for his books. She had read and re-read them, trying to understand this strange distant man whose eyes held the icy faraway look of the mountains he loved so much. She could not forget him—but how could she tell Nick all this?

'Wake up, Lauren.' Nick's impatient voice jerked her back to the present. 'You haven't fastened your belt yet.'

'Sorry,' she murmured, her hands fumbling

with the lock.

'Oh, let me,' Nick said quickly, leaning towards her, and taking the belt from her awkward hands.

Once again the impersonal voice interrupted the chatter in the plane. 'We are now approaching Paradise Island,' it said. 'We hope you will enjoy your stay.'

Lauren stiffened to attention and turned instantly to the man by her side. 'Nick, I didn't know we were going to Paradise Island.'

Nick looked amused. 'Surely you did!'

She shook her head vigorously. 'No. I knew it was the Island Hotel, but I didn't know what island.'

'Does it matter?' he asked.

She looked troubled, one hand flying to touch her ash-blonde hair nervously. 'I don't know, Nick. It might. You see, Deborah Lindstrom—she's one of my young pupils—well, she and her mother are coming to Paradise Island for a holiday. They might recognize me.'

Nick did not look alarmed. 'I very much doubt it. You look so different,' he said reassuringly.

Lauren took her powder compact out of her white handbag and studied her face carefully in the mirror. 'No, I don't look like me at all,' she said rather wistfully.

Nick laughed outright. 'Of course you don't.' He lowered his voice and added:

4

'Remember you're now Natalie Natal, the famous dancer, and you are no longer little Lauren Roubin, who teaches ballet dancing to kids.'

Worriedly, Lauren looked in the mirror at the sophisticated face staring back at her. Honestly, she thought, she much preferred her own face, but then, as Nick had reminded her, she was taking his wife's place. Nick's wife, Natalie, was still in hospital after a serious operation. Lauren had known both Nick and Natalie for several years; she liked them both and was glad to be able to help them out. Looking at Nick, she told herself that he was so kind and helpful that she could not really feel worried about the near future. Nick would always help her cope with any situation, no matter how difficult it might prove to be.

'Honey child,' Nick said, his voice urgent, 'look.'

Lauren obeyed. The plane was circling as it came lower and lower. Below them, they could see the cleared airstrip and the air sock waving in the breeze. Lauren had a vague impression of white buildings, green grass and then there was a gentle bump and Nick was saying: 'Nicely done.'

Looking out of the window, Lauren's eyes were dazzled by the blinding sunshine and the white buildings. She saw the beautiful wide beds of flowers of every imaginable colour—vivid reds, brilliant orange, golden yellow, deep blue, white. It was all so very beautiful, and yet, absurd as it was, she felt disappointed. It was all so unreal, so artificial—like a stage backdrop, too beautiful to be true. Rather like her new self, she told herself unhappily. She liked things—and people—to be natural, even if it did mean losing some of the glamour.

People all round them were rising and gathering their things together, so Lauren began to draw on her gloves and picked up her handbag. Nick's hand pulled her back into her seat as she rose.

'No need to rush, honey,' he said. 'We must act like seasoned travellers.'

She looked at him unhappily. 'Nick, I'm scared. Suppose I let you down? I know I'll never dance like Natalie. Suppose someone finds out I'm not really your dancing partner but just a substitute?' Her hands felt sticky with fear.

Nick smiled at her. 'Calm down, my dear. Panic over. You'll do fine. You're a very good dancer—a natural, in fact; you'll soon learn. We've only been practising together for six days and you've made rapid strides.' His smile was kind. 'No one will know you. If you're worrying about this Mrs. Lindstrom, I doubt if she has seen you more than once? I thought not. I bet she didn't even look at her child's dancing teacher. You'd be small beer to her.'

Lauren relaxed, telling herself that Nick was right. Mrs. Lindstrom was a wealthy socialite;

she had only called once for her child after dancing class, and then she had been in a great hurry. Deborah, now, was different . .

Waiting in the plane, Lauren could remember vividly that day in the basement studio of the Cartwright School of Dancing where she taught. The yellow fog of a November day had come creeping through the cracks in the closed window, the room was like an ice-box and the children, in their little tutus, had heard the tinkling notes of the piano die away and had lined up for their usual walk past as they curtseyed and wished Lauren goodbye. How sedately they had walked, their tutus swinging, their faces very earnest, and then Deborah, last in the line, had forgotten dignity and had rushed at Lauren with her small freckled face radiant.

'I'm going abwoad with my mummy,' she had cried, hugging Lauren round the waist.

Although Lauren always tried to conceal it, Deborah was her favourite. The shy awkward child with the plain face and the straggly hair had seemed to blossom since she started learning ballet, as if gaining grace and confidence as she improved. So Lauren had hugged Deborah back, delighting in her happiness but a little surprised that Mrs. Lindstrom would take the child with her. Deborah's nannie, in her neat grey uniform, had joined them and had told Lauren wryly— after she sent the little girl away to get her outdoor shoes—that she was sorry for the child.

'I'm not going with them,' she had said. 'I'm due for a holiday and am going to Norway to ski. The poor little brat is being taken along as ammunition,' she had said bitterly, and then looked ashamed. 'Maybe I shouldn't say that, but Mrs. L. doesn't care one bit for the child.' She might have said more, but Deborah had returned at that moment, her face still excited.

'We're going to Pawadise Island, Miss Woubin,' she had said, her smile revealing the gaps in her teeth. 'I'm going to be vewy good and I'm going with my mummy.'

Lauren had often found herself remembering the little conversation and wondering just what the nannie had meant by 'ammunition'.

\*       \*       \*

Nick's hand shaking her arm jerked Lauren back to the present and the plane. 'Wakey-wakey, child,' Nick was saying. 'Come back from that secret place of yours. Time to get moving.'

Obediently, Lauren rose and followed him. As they stepped out of the plane, the heat seemed to rush to embrace them with sticky arms. The blinding sunlight made her stumble, and Nick's hand was immediately under her elbow.

'It is hot!' she gasped.

'Well, what did you expect?' Nick asked, laughing down at her dismayed face. 'You'll soon get used to it.'

The thick white coat she had been so glad of in wet, cold London was now too heavy, so Nick helped her out of it. Lauren smoothed down the elegant blue silk suit and put up a hand to adjust her blue feather hat as she stared around with curious eyes.

There were a number of cars being filled with passengers and luggage. Several neatly uniformed, dark-skinned men were walking about briskly. There were groups of people, chatting and laughing, and several men with cameras were hurrying from group to group, and always—just like a background—there was the deep green of the grass, the dazzling white of the buildings, and the great blue cloudless sky.

Nick leaned towards her and whispered in her ear: 'Wipe that dewy-eyed look of excitement off your face, honey child. You look about sixteen. Where, for Pete's sake, are your sunglasses? Put 'em on and try to look blasé!'

Blushing, Lauren fumbled in her handbag, found her sunglasses and took refuge behind them. Instantly the scene changed, losing some of its beauty but also losing a lot of the artificiality of the vivid colours. How did you look bored, she wondered, when you were so thrilled?

Nick took her arm and they strolled along as he said softly:

'Look as if you expect people to stand and gape at your beauty. They should, and they will. You look ravishing, honey child. Good enough to eat, and don't you forget it.'

She recognized the concern in his voice and smiled at him.

'I'll do my best, Nick,' she promised.

The Press photographers came rushing up. Obediently she stood still as cameras clicked and whirred. She tilted her head, gazing round her slowly as if critical of what she saw, heard Nick's swiftly smothered chuckle and knew she was doing all right. She glanced down at her elegant blue silk suit, put up a languid hand to touch her elaborately-set hair, and then Nick was grabbing her arm, muttering angrily:

'Stop acting like a stork!'

She understood immediately, and her face felt on fire as she hastily lowered her foot and planted it firmly on the ground. She had an awful habit of rubbing one foot against the other leg—it dated back to the time of the accident which had caused her to give up her dream of becoming a ballerina. It was a habit her family and Miss Cartwright were always scolding her about, a habit she seemed unable to overcome. Still flushed, she obediently turned sideways in answer to a photographer's request. She smiled at him as he thanked her and then he was gone.

Nick's arm tightened round her shoulders for a moment.

'Sorry I snapped your head off,' he said contritely. 'But I didn't want them to film you standing on one leg. What gives, honeychild?'

Lauren looked at him miserably.

'I never know I'm doing it,' she confessed miserably. 'I think it started when I hurt my leg. It used to ache all the time, and somehow it seemed to ease it if I rubbed my foot up and down my calf. I—I usually do it when I'm nervous or tired.'

Nick was laughing. 'One thing, your long full dance gowns should hide any little trick like that, so we needn't worry. It's a funny sort of habit—' He laughed down at her. 'You're a strange girl altogether, going off into your dreams, never seeming to be in this world, always surprising me.'

As they walked along together, Nick was glancing about him as if not sure what to do next, and then an African chauffeur in spotless white uniform came to take their luggage and lead the way to an open cream car.

The road was wide and winding as it slowly climbed towards the huge white building that dominated the island. Lauren caught exciting glimpses of blue sea in the distance as majestic palms bowed their heads gracefully. There were wide beds of flowers everywhere. The air was soft and warm on her cheeks.

11

Nick told her it was a very exclusive hotel. 'You practically need an introduction before you can make a booking there. Part of the hotel is the luxury side with a smooth wide beach on which to parade your talents if you're searching for a wealthy husband,' he said, his eyes twinkling. 'But I think you'd better use the family beach. You're too young to cope with the roaming wolves. In any case, I gather the family beach is the nicest, softer sand, and has more shade and safer swimming. The hotel welcomes families but has chalets for them, and as hot meals are served individually in the chalets three times a day, there's no need for the children or their parents to go into the hotel unless they want to. A sort of home from home, but boy, what it costs!' Nick paused to whistle softly.

'What will I have to do?' Lauren asked rather nervously.

'Dance, chiefly. You may be asked to give some dancing lessons, but I'll be around, so you'll have nothing to worry about. You can have the morning off and it can be yours completely. At three o'clock each day we'll practise, and afterwards you'll go to the hairdresser, and then, in the evening, we dance. Three dances a night.' He pursed his mouth thoughtfully. 'We must put on a good show, honey child. This could lead to bigger and better things. Never know who you'll meet in a hotel like this. I was thinking that in the

12

morning, if you promise to stick to the family beach, you could be yourself if you like. No make-up, your own clothes. Would that help?' He smiled at her and she hugged his arm impulsively.

'You really are a darling, Nick. You think of everything,' she told him gratefully.

He looked grave. 'I hope I have. It's a pretty big responsibility looking after a kid like you. Natalie would give me hell if anything happened to you.'

'What could happen?'

He frowned. 'You're so terribly young. You think everyone is good. You're just an innocent little ignoramus.'

'I am not!' Lauren said indignantly. She was getting tired of being constantly told that she was young. 'I'm twenty-one and I know all about—'

Nick was laughing. 'The birds, the bees and the butterflies? I bet you do, for you have a sensible sort of mother. All the same, you've never had to cope with a drunk or a man who . . .' He shrugged. 'Skip it, honey. I promised Natalie I'd keep an eye on you.'

Lauren's temper had vanished. 'I promised the same,' she told him.

Nick posed, pretending to look arrogant, running his hand over his smooth dark hair. She thought for a moment how very good-looking he was with his lean humorous face and dark laughing eyes.

'I take it that Natalie is afraid that my fatal charm . . .'

'It's the girls she doesn't trust,' Lauren said.

His face clouded. 'How I wish she wasn't so jealous and possessive. Look, Lauren, I have to be polite to the women and—'

'She can't help it,' Lauren said gently. 'She loves you so much.'

They were passing groups of Africans wearing bright clothes, with small plump children with white-toothed smiles in their shining dark faces.

'I hope to make some money on the side,' Nick said abruptly. 'Acting as a gigolo and giving dancing lessons. I plan to give Natalie the holiday of her life when she's well enough to enjoy it.' He sighed. 'It's funny how many people think this is an easy life. If only they knew how very exhausting, boring and predatory women can be! Ah, here we are,' he said as they drove through the wide open wrought iron gates. 'Quite a place.'

It certainly was. Lauren gazed up at the great white building with respect. It positively screamed luxury and great wealth. Each room appeared to have a balcony with a pink and white striped canopy. There were window boxes on the ground floor, but she recognized none of the flowers. They must be tropical, she thought, and wondered who she could ask, because she knew her father would be interested, for he was a keen gardener.

14

The car stopped and they went up the wide white steps and into an opulent hall that stretched away into apparent infinity because of the mirrors that threw back reflections. Lauren's feet sank into the thick, vividly green carpet. There was a curving gracious staircase painted white and gold, and comfortable armchairs. She stared at a girl—tall, slim, lovely, a handful of blue feathers on ash-blonde hair, an elegant blue suit, long slim legs ending in high-heeled white shoes, eager eyes hidden behind dark glasses, and she was amazed that it could be a reflection of herself. She turned to Nick and saw that his face was grim, and she could sense the tenseness in his suddenly still body as a tall woman swept towards them.

A beautiful woman, and yet . . . yet there was something lacking in her face. Was it the lack of warmth? Her eyes were hard and shrewd, her mouth a thin determined line. Her jet-black hair was knotted low on her neck. She wore an exquisitely-cut black suit, with a cascade of white ruffles at her neck and a diamond spray on the lapel of her coat.

'Welcome to the Island Hotel,' she said in a flat voice. 'You must be . . .' She paused, her eyes running over Nick's slender tall figure, his well-cut dark suit, his black smooth hair.

Nick gave a jerky little bow. 'How right you are. Yes, we are the dancers.' He sounded ironical. 'Natalie and Nicholas Natal, at your

15

service. How charming of you to spare time to welcome us personally, Miss . . .' His voice was very faintly insolent.

The woman's blank eyes seemed to come to life. 'I am Miss Hunter,' she said arrogantly. 'I manage the hotel and engage all staff.' She ignored Lauren completely, her eyes concentrated on Nick's face. 'You should go down well with the ladies.' Her voice was as insolent as his.

Lauren stared at them unhappily and looked away, trying to detach herself. Why must they behave like this? As if they were a couple of dogs sparring before a fight started.

She was suddenly afraid. How would they get on if Miss Hunter disliked them from the beginning? Natalie had told her about their experiences at different hotels and that you had to behave arrogantly or you were treated as dirt. Was that why Nick was starting this way?

She was really frightened by now, sure she had made a mistake in saying she would help Nick and Miss Cartwright. It could only lead to humiliation. 'Have fun,' Natalie had said. It didn't look as if it was going to be much fun . . .

It had all began on that same foggy day after Deborah and her nannie had gone off. Lauren had been sent for by Miss Cartwright, the owner and Principal of the Cartwright School of Dancing. She was a tyrannical woman of seventy-eight, with terrific ambition and

16

energy, and a habit of ruling her staff with the proverbial rod of iron hidden in a velvet glove.

In some fear, for Miss Cartwright only sent for you if she was angry, Lauren had gone to see her, and had been surprised to find that Miss Cartwright was asking a favour of her.

It seemed that two of their ballroom dancers were booked to spend three months at the famous Island Hotel and that one of them, Natalie, was ill. Nick, Natalie's husband and partner, was in the room, and he told Lauren of Natalie's sudden spasm of pain and of the specialist's decision that an immediate operation was imperative and that it might be months before she could dance again.

'I hate leaving her,' Nick had said worriedly, 'but at least I'll be with her until after the op, and a job is a job, after all.'

'Of course it is,' Miss Cartwright had snapped. 'The dance must go on. I have never let down a client yet and I don't mean to start now.'

Nick and Natalie Natal were, in reality, Sam and Betty Johnson, but they had bowed to Miss Cartwright's love of alliteration. Lauren had often been to their flat in Bayswater for coffee and a chat.

In the end, Miss Cartwright had bluntly asked Lauren if she would replace Natalie and go to the Island Hotel with Nick.

Lauren had been startled and afraid. 'I've never done any exhibition dancing, Miss

17

Cartwright. Natalie is so good . . . I've got a bad knee, you know.' She had tried to think up excuses, but she knew it was useless. When Miss Cartwright made up her mind . . . Nick was smiling at her, and he had been encouraging.

'Of course you could do it, Lauren. You danced with James when Josie was ill.'

Lauren had shuddered, remembering James's impatience.

'And your knee hasn't troubled you for months,' Miss Cartwright had pointed out.

'Look, honey child,' Nick had said. He called all the girls 'honey child'; he said it was easier than trying to remember their names! 'We're good friends. Three months of being cooped up in a deadly luxury hotel on a small island can try the patience of saints, but we get on well. I'll teach you. I can make the dances seem more dramatic than they really are, at first, until you get the hang of things. You're a good dancer, and I need your help badly.' There had been a desperate note in his voice that she could not resist.

'All right,' she agreed reluctantly. 'I'll do my best, but . . .'

Miss Cartwright had beamed and said that she had always known Lauren was a good girl, and Nick had heaved a sigh of relief and began to make plans instantly. Six hectic days had followed. Six days, packed with hours of practising, of Nick being very patient and

18

encouraging as he taught her the different lifts, how she must help, brace herself; how to dramatize the full skirts of the lovely dance gowns. Days of her muscles aching and her head throbbing; of hours of trying on the beautiful gowns provided by Miss Cartwright for Natalie's professional wardrobe. Then a quick visit to Hastings and her parents; their excitement and her forebodings, her sister's wide-eyed envy of her good fortune; then several visits to poor Natalie in hospital—a wan, unhappy Natalie whose eyes were feverish with anxiety.

'I hate Nick going without me, but I'd sooner he went with you than any other girl I know,' she said. 'I can trust you, Lauren.'

'You can trust Nick, Natalie,' Lauren assured her. 'He worships the ground you walk on.'

'It isn't Nick,' Natalie had whispered wearily. 'It's the other girls. Even when I'm with him, they try to grab him.'

'I won't let them,' Lauren had promised. 'I'll guard him as a mother guards her young!'

One thing, that had made poor Natalie laugh. 'Bless you,' she had said. 'Have fun.'

Have fun! Here she was, in this luxury hotel, already worried about what was going to happen. She looked round the lofty spacious hall with the gold and white pillars, the deep recess where the reception counter was, through the wide open doors which framed a

19

scene of great beauty—the velvet-smooth green lawns, the wide beds of vividly coloured flowers, even a distant glimpse of the blue sea.

Suddenly she caught her breath, her hand flying to her throat nervously as she stared at the man walking towards her.

It could not be!

But it was!

She drew a long shuddering breath, feeling her whole body tingle with excitement. It was Roland Harvey himself!

Here, in this hotel. It didn't seem possible. The great Roland Harvey.

He was just as she remembered him, only much more so—tall with a hard leanness that promised well-trained muscles. His eyes still had that faraway look as if he was searching for the distant mountains. He was close enough for her to see that his eyes were a mixture of blue and grey. How lightly he walked, how straight his back was! He had been a soldier; she knew that, from reading his books. His personality, close to, was almost overwhelming. He seemed to throw off waves of virility. All the people around were looking at him, the women especially. He wore a very well-cut tropical suit with a spotless white silk shirt and a grey silk cravat, and his brown shoes were gleaming. How truly elegant he looked, and yet how very masculine.

He walked quite close to her as he passed, but he did not turn his head or make any sign

20

that he had seen her. He looked like a man who could make instant decisions and never be wrong. Somehow he did not look like a married man. He looked too remote to be mixed up with human emotions. Yet that woman in the lecture hall had said he was crazy about children, especially little girls. It was hard to imagine Roland Harvey crazy about anyone.

She felt uncertain and horribly young. She was sure that if she had been Mrs. Lindstrom she could have made use of the chance—that she could have stopped him with a casual remark, or told him how much she enjoyed his books . . .

She was suddenly aware that Nick was speaking to her.

'Please, honey child, wake up! Miss Hunter will take you to your room.' His voice was stiff. With anger? 'She wants to talk to you alone.'

Miss Hunter looked a little flushed. Had she lost the first round and was she resenting it? Lauren wondered uneasily.

'I kept speaking to you,' Miss Hunter said impatiently. 'Are you deaf?'

Nick answered for her, with a light laugh. 'Only day-dreaming as usual.'

Somehow Lauren spoke, and followed Miss Hunter's stiff uncompromising back to the lift. Her thoughts were whirling. Fancy—Roland Harvey, staying here. Would she, perhaps, have the chance to meet him? Talk to him? If

21

he liked dancing . . . but that was fantastic. She could not imagine Roland Harvey unbending enough to dance. But how wonderful if . . .

She followed Miss Hunter into the lift. At the fifth floor they got out, then walked down the corridor, Lauren's feet sinking into the thick carpet, and then Miss Hunter threw open the door of a room and stood back.

'I trust that you will find this satisfactory,' she said, her voice thick with sarcasm.

The first thing Lauren saw was the wide open windows and the wonderful view. The blue sea, waving palm trees, white sands. It was like a film. It looked far too beautiful to be real.

The second impression she got was of the brightness of everything—the dazzling sunshine, the white curtains —white furniture . . .

And two single beds!

She caught her breath in dismay. Why, of course, she was supposed to be Nick's wife! She bit her lip nervously. She had never thought of this—and she was sure that Nick hadn't, either.

'Now what's wrong?' Miss Hunter snapped. 'Perhaps you want a private bathroom?'

Lauren turned to face the cold, beautiful woman. Without realizing it, she held out her hands imploringly. 'Could—couldn't we have two rooms?' she stammered.

Miss Hunter's face changed. She was scowling. 'Don't tell me you're the sort of

22

married couple who insist on separate rooms, Our usual practice is—'

Lauren's face felt on fire. Everything was forgotten but this one embarrassing problem. 'We're not married,' she said. What else was there to say?

She watched the cold, beautiful face grow scarlet, saw the dark eyes flash as Miss Hunter's calm vanished. 'You must be married,' she almost hissed. 'We specifically engaged a married couple.' She was very angry indeed, could hardly speak. 'It cannot be tolerated. Miss Cartwright knew very well that we will only employ married couples as dancers. She has broken the contract, and I—'

Lauren felt frozen with shock and horror. She had not expected this. 'It wasn't Miss Cartwright's fault,' she began.

Miss Hunter was not listening. She was turning away.

'You will not be permitted to stay. You will both have to return to England.' She turned round to stare at Lauren, her eyes cold with dislike. 'I know that the owner of the hotel will not permit you to stay.'

'The owner?' Lauren said.

Miss Hunter nodded. 'Yes, the owner. I manage the hotel, but he has very decided views. Very decided indeed. I know he will make you return to England immediately. He . . .'

'He?' Lauren said as Miss Hunter paused,

her face contorted with fresh anger.

Miss Hunter's voice was bitter as she replied. 'Yes, he. The one and only, famous Roland Harvey.'

## CHAPTER TWO

Roland Harvey. Roland Harvey!

The name thundered through Lauren's head as she stared in dismay at Miss Hunter's angry face.

So this was how she was to meet him—for the first and perhaps the only time in her life. She could just imagine the steely coldness of his disapproval. He would dismiss their little deception as *deliberate trickery.* She shivered.

'Please, Miss Hunter—' she began.

The beautiful face was hard. 'It's no good trying to talk me round . . .'

And then, miraculously, Nick was there, taking charge. Lauren saw instantly by his face that, like her, he had forgotten this aspect of their plan, and he smiled at her reassuringly and then turned to devote himself to the angry Miss Hunter. With a strange humility, he was, he said, going to throw himself on her mercy. His wife was very ill . . .

Vaguely Lauren listened to their conversation, but she stood a little apart, fearful to say anything lest it be the wrong thing. Her thoughts were on Roland Harvey. How awful to have to face him and his wrath.

And then, suddenly, everything was all right. Miss Hunter expressed herself as satisfied with their explanation, and as there were extenuating circumstances, said she would overlook the deception, but to simplify matters, it would be best for Lauren to continue to pretend to be Natalie Natal. Then she took Nick away, to arrange about a bedroom for him.

Lauren went to sit on her balcony for a while, for she felt exhausted. She still could not believe that everything was all right. She had been so sure that they would be packed off home like naughty schoolchildren in disgrace!

A pretty little olive-skinned maid called Claudia came to help her unpack. Lauren changed into a simple cotton frock and hurried to join Nick in the deserted ballroom, where she was introduced to the members of the small orchestra and she and Nick had a quick work-out. They were doing an easy dance first, to break her in, Nick said teasingly, and luckily she knew the three dances well and there was nothing tricky about them to be remembered.

All the same, as she got ready that evening, her fingers seemed to be all thumbs and she was glad of Claudia's help. The little maid's slanting eyes widened with excitement as she helped Lauren into the gold satin gown.

What a day it had been! A day of

excitement and fear, of soaring to the heights with excitement when she saw Roland Harvey walking across the hotel hall . . . a day of fear when she thought they would have to leave this wonderful spot and that she might have to face Roland Harvey's anger.

She stared anxiously at her mirrored reflection. Was that really her? The hairdresser, a funny little Frenchman, had first given her hair a gold rinse and then had set it so that it clung smoothly to her head, making her look like a faun.

The gown, of course, was out of this world. Her hands caressed the heavy satin folds. She gazed at the strapless draped bodice and deceptively straight-looking skirt that hung in demure folds until she whirled round before the mirror and the huge width of it spun in a circle of beauty and then, as she stood still, fell again into the same straight graceful folds.

She was to wear no jewellery, Nick had said. He had told her what make-up she was to use, and her eyes were touched with golden eye-shadow, her mouth a shade of red which toned with the gold.

Nick called for her, standing in the corridor, immaculate in his white shirt and black tails. 'You look really lovely, honey child,' he said slowly. 'Of course you do look artificial,' he added, with his uncanny knack of reading her thoughts, 'but who wants to look at a country lass with roses in her cheeks in a ballroom?'

He had her laughing as they hurried along luxuriously-carpeted corridors, and down in the lift to the ballroom. It was no longer quiet and empty—a wave of laughter and voices surged through the open doors and screened windows that were wide open to the hot night.

'I'm scared,' Lauren whispered, her mouth dry, as they waited.

His hands were warm on her bare arms for a moment. 'Relax, honey child,' he said gently. 'I know you'll be all right.' He bent and kissed her mouth very lightly. 'I know.'

She smiled shakily. She knew he was trying to give her courage. He had never kissed her before and she knew it meant nothing. Vaguely she thought she saw Miss Hunter hovering, but the next moment the drums rolled, Nick took her hand to lead her forward and she forgot everything else. She heard a deep voice announcing them and she gazed round. The lights were low and the voices suddenly stilled—the silence was frightening, the faces just a shapeless blur. A pool of golden light fell on them and Nick smiled at her, taking her in his arms as the orchestra began to play.

Immediately she forgot her nervousness as she became lost in the intricacies of the dance, the need to follow him exactly, the timing, the tensing of her body at the right moment, the sudden fluidity as she spun round slowly to dramatize the great circle of the skirt.

As they took their first bow, the applause

rippled down the ballroom and grew to a crescendo. Her cheeks flushed, her eyes like stars, Lauren had to curtsey again and again. Finally they were allowed to escape to the balcony, where they were to wait until their next dance was due.

Leaning against the stone parapet, Lauren drew in deep breaths of the warm night air. How wonderfully, unbelievably lovely it all was! It was like being transplanted to another world—a fairyland. The moon was a golden ball in the midnight-blue sky and threw a golden pathway across the lagoon. The palm trees cast shadows over the smooth lawns. From behind them drifted the sounds of laughter and voices.

'You were wonderful, Lauren,' Nick said with unusual gravity.

She swung round to stare at him, her eyes wide with excitement. 'Was I really, Nick? Was I really all right? I was terrified at first, but once we began to dance . . .'

'You were perfect.' He was walking up and down restlessly. Suddenly he stopped. 'Tell me the truth, Lauren. Didn't you enjoy it?'

She stared at him. 'Why, yes, Nick, I did,' she said wonderingly. 'I loved every moment of it. It was just that first bad moment.'

'You always get butterflies inside you at the start,' he told her. 'I still do, but they go.'

'Oh yes, they went. I always love dancing with you, Nick, and then—then when they all clapped and shouted . . . Yes, I got a real thrill out of it.'

Nick stubbed out his cigarette. 'The bug has bitten you, honey child.' He laughed. 'You'll never be able to go back to teaching kids how to dance.'

'Won't I?' She was suddenly worried. Was this the sort of life she wanted? Subject to the whims of a difficult, perhaps bad-tempered hotel manager? And who could she get for a partner? Someone like that terrible James? And yet it was an exciting way to live, and what a wonderful chance to see the world, wear lovely gowns, and always have the thrill of dancing.

Their next two dances were also easy—a slow, languorous tango and a romantic waltz. It was as she curtseyed after the third dance that Lauren saw Roland Harvey.

He was sitting alone at a table—a man with broad shoulders and an austere face who looked as out of place in his surroundings as she felt she must look with her unnatural hair and face. He sat bolt upright and he looked horribly disapproving. Perhaps he thought dancing was too flippant—perhaps he didn't approve of the way they danced?

In the small ante-room where their dinner was served, Lauren and Nick discussed the evening.

'Did you see Roland Harvey?' Nick asked. 'He looked pretty sour. Miss Hunter tells me he can be very difficult. One thing, I think we're quite safe, for you're not likely to run into him, honey child.'

'Aren't I?' Lauren looked up from her prawn cocktail. She felt suddenly bleak. 'Why ever not?'

Nick chuckled. 'Because he runs a mile when he sees a pretty girl. Marriage doesn't come into his scheme of living, and they're all after him—more so than ever since his uncle left him a fortune as well as this hotel.'

Several things seemed to click in Lauren's mind and dovetail like the pieces of a jigsaw puzzle.

The conversation she had overheard in the lecture hall when the two women had been discussing Roland Harvey and had said he would do anything for small girls . . . Deborah's nannie who had remarked that Mrs. Lindstrom was looking for a wealthy husband and was taking Deborah along as 'ammunition'. Could Mrs. Lindstrom have her eyes on Roland Harvey?

Lauren was instantly ashamed of such a catty thought, but it had reminded her of something.

'I hope Mrs. Lindstrom won't recognize me,' she said.

Nick helped himself to lobster. 'I doubt it. She's only seen you once, and you look so very different now.' He frowned. 'Maybe it would be wiser if you stuck to the role of Natalie all

30

the time . . .' He paused, seeing the dismayed look on Lauren's face and he smiled. 'All right, honey child, but remember you must never get the two girls mixed up. When you are Lauren Roubin, slip out the back way and keep to the family beach. When you are Natalie Natal, stay in the luxury setting and act like Natalie.' He nodded as the waiter refilled his glass with wine. 'And, Lauren, remember that every day at three o'clock we practise.'

'I'm like Cinderella, only for me the clock strikes at three,' Lauren said, and laughed.

Nick laughed as well. 'Never forget it, or else!' He pretended to scowl.

*     *     *

Lauren slept deeply that night, exhausted mentally as well as physically. She was surprised to see the time when she opened her eyes and saw Claudia there with a tray of tea. She did not want to waste one moment of the lovely day, so she showered and dressed while waiting for her breakfast of coffee and rolls, which she ate on the balcony. High up, she had a lovely view of the island and could plainly see the 'family' lagoon Nick had described. It looked lovely—the narrow strip of land running out in a half-circle in the sea, with the tall palms waving slowly. Laughter and voices drifted up to her.

Looking in her mirror, she smiled at herself.

31

It was good to be Lauren Roubin again. She had washed the gold rinse and lacquer out of her hair and now it swung to her shoulders, curling under, in gleaming ash-blonde silkiness. She had applied sunburn lotion to her face, neck and shoulders because Nick had warned her against getting burned. She wore her new green swimsuit and green and white striped shorts, a white shirt, and a white towelling coat. How very very young she looked, she thought discontentedly, and then reminded herself that it was a good thing in a way, for no one would connect one so young-looking with the sophisticated painted beauty that was Natalie Natal. As a last disguise, she wore dark glasses, then she used the service lift to get down to the ground floor and out through a small side entrance so that there would be no likelihood of meeting Deborah or her mother. It would be terrible if she met them and they recognized her. Despite the great heat, she shivered. She could not bear it if Roland Harvey sent her home!

Outside, the bright sunlight made her pause for a moment, not sure which way to go. There were men and women and children, all wearing sun-suits or swimsuits, wandering about. It was all utterly lovely—so very colourful. The blaze of the flowers, the deep green of the well-cared-for lawns, all the colours of the gay clothes. On a large lawn, there was a Chinese pagoda type of summer-house. Everywhere there was chatter and laughter, and sweet exotic scents from the flowers.

Lauren decided that she would follow the way most of the children were going, for surely that should lead to the family beach? She could see the small village of white chalets and catch glimpses of the pretty dark-skinned maids cleaning them.

She had taken only a few steps when something hurtled against her, clutching her, crying in a familiar voice: 'Miss Woubin, Miss Woubin!'

Catching her breath with dismay, Lauren stared down into the upturned, tear-stained face of Deborah.

'Why, Deborah darling!' Lauren said, trying to sound pleased.

A shadow seemed to block out the sunlight, and Lauren shivered as she saw that it was Mrs. Lindstrom herself—tall, slim, incredibly elegant in a lilac-coloured silk sun-suit, her eyes hidden by dark glasses but her voice expressing her surprise.

'It is Miss Roubin, isn't it? I certainly didn't expect to see you here, and when Deborah said she saw you—what on earth are you doing here?' Mrs. Lindstrom asked, her voice tart. Fortunately she gave Lauren no time to answer, for she went on: 'Oh, of course, I remember. I heard they were arranging to give the children dancing lessons. I suppose that's why. This must seem a great change to you, Miss Roubin.' There was a hint of condescension in her voice.

'Oh, it is, Mrs. Lindstrom,' Lauren said eagerly, grateful for the fact that Mrs. Lindstrom seemed to have answered her own question to her complete satisfaction. 'It is wonderful—out of this world.'

Deborah was clutching her hand tightly. 'Come and see the sands and the tiny shells and—'

'Don't bother Miss Roubin, monkey,' Mrs. Lindstrom said sharply.

The joy was wiped off the child's freckled face. Her lower lip trembled.

'But, Mummy,' Deborah said wistfully, 'Miss Woubin likes being bovered, don't you, Miss Woubin?'

Lauren laughed and smiled at Mrs. Lindstrom. 'Deborah is right. Might I borrow her, Mrs. Lindstrom? It's my first day here and I'm a bit lost.'

The quick relief Mrs. Lindstrom betrayed was instantly hidden. 'If you're sure she won't be a nuisance. Her lunch hour is twelve o'clock and then she has an hour's rest.'

'I'll bring her back in good time,' Lauren promised.

Deborah, still clutching her hand, was jumping about excitedly, the words tumbling out of her mouth as they walked along the wide pathway that led to the lagoon and beach.

34

They kept meeting people Deborah knew, and she kept saying: 'This is my Miss Woubin. She teaches me dancing.'

Lauren was not sure whether to laugh or cry. Miss Roubin would certainly be well-known now! Was it going to be possible, after all, to keep Lauren and Natalie as two separate people? Supposing Mrs. Lindstrom recognized her tonight as she danced?

The fragrance of jasmine teased her nose, the brilliant crimson of the poinsettias delighted her eyes, and Deborah's sticky fingers clinging to hers promised companionship, so Lauren decided to forget her worry for the time being. She could talk to Nick about it that afternoon. For the moment, she was going to enjoy herself. Just in case . . . just in case they were not allowed to stay!

The wide half-circle of beach was dazzling white in the bright sunshine. Huge striped red and white sunshades were propped in the sand, tilted to throw welcome shade. With the air of an old-timer, Deborah picked one up from a pile and told Lauren they would go over to a certain big rock where the best shells were found. Lauren looked obediently in the direction indicated and saw a strangely-shaped rock, balanced on one point precariously, reminding her irresistibly of a ballerina learning to stand on her points.

'Does your mummy bring you here?' she asked Deborah curiously, as the warm sand filtered through her sandals and between her toes.

Deborah looked startled. 'Oh, no, my mummy hates the sand. I come with my friend.' She said it importantly. Lauren wondered who was Deborah's 'friend'. Probably a little girl of the same age group.

Lauren spread her white beach coat on the hot sand and lay down, and Deborah struggled to stick the sunshade in the sand. With Lauren's aid, they managed, and tilted it to keep the sun off Lauren's face.

'I'll get you some shells,' Deborah promised, and raced off towards the water's edge where the sea trickled in so very gently, forming tiny scallops of white.

Lauren relaxed, closing her eyes, feeling the blessed warmth of the sun on her body. Oh, what bliss! And how very different from London in a fog! How lucky she was . . . if only her luck held. If only Deborah and Mrs. Lindstrom hadn't seen her . .

She must have dozed, for Deborah's shrill little voice awoke her from her dreams. Lauren opened her eyes and stared up into the face of a man.

A man with grey-blue eyes, a man with dark red, disciplined hair. A man with a stern mouth who unexpectedly smiled.

'I'm afraid we woke you up,' he said crisply.

Lauren struggled to wake up properly. There had been nothing hostile in the voice, yet Nick had said Roland Harvey hated and avoided young women.

She sat up, staring at him stupidly, rubbing her hand over her sleepy eyes, trying to concentrate. His suntanned body was clad in white shorts and he had a large red and white towel over one shoulder. Even as she stared at him, he slid on his dark glasses and she could no longer see the expression in his eyes.

'I'm sorry if we disturbed you,' he said a little stiffly.

'Of course not,' she said, suddenly confused as she realized at long last she was actually speaking to Roland Harvey himself. 'I'm afraid I was drowsy. I didn't mean to be rude, Mr. Harvey.'

He smiled, a warm human smile that amazed her. Somehow she had always thought of him as rather inhuman—not quite the same as the rest of the people in the world. She had also thought he would be hard, cold.

'Of course you weren't rude. I know how strange one feels when one first wakes up. You know who I am?'

'Well, of course. I—I saw you in London . . . you were lecturing . . .'

'You came to one of my lectures?' He sounded surprised.

'Yes, and—and I've read your books.'

'May I?' he asked, and taking her silence as consent, sat down on the sand by her side. 'Well, Miss Roubin—' He paused, still staring at her. If only she could see the expression in those hidden eyes.

Stop being scared, she told herself. He knows you as Deborah's friend, the little dancing teacher, Miss Roubin. He hasn't any idea that he saw you dancing last night. Don't panic, as Nick would say.

He was stretched out on the sand by her side, leaning on one elbow.

'Don't tell me you actually *read* my books?' he said, and there was a strange smile on his mouth.

Her cheeks burned. 'But I have read them,' she said indignantly, stung by his amusement. 'I'll be honest . . . I didn't want to go to this lecture, but I went to please a girl who shares my room at the hostel, and I—I enjoyed the lecture so much that next day I went to the library and got out your books.' He was still gazing at her, but she struggled on. He had to believe her, she thought confusedly. Somehow it was terribly important to make him know she was telling the truth. 'I liked the book about the mountains best. You really made me feel the excitement of it—the struggle—the challenge . . .'

'I believe you're telling the truth,' he said, his voice surprised.

'Of course I am,' she said, suddenly cross. 'Why should I lie to you?'

'Why not?' he asked. 'Plenty of people do.' He smiled. This time it was the sort of smile she hated—sarcastic, sceptical. 'My dear Miss Roubin,' he went on, seeming to bite his words in half, so crisply did he speak. 'If you knew the number of pretty young women who tell me they've read my books and yet who couldn't name a single one of them, you'd understand my surprise.'

She sat up, her cheeks red, her eyes flashing. 'I'm not lying to you. You can test me. Go on. I'd like you to. Ask me the titles of your books, what they are about . . .'

'I really don't think that's necessary,' he said stiffly.

'Oh, but it is,' Lauren said earnestly. What was the matter with her? she wondered. How confused she felt. 'I've read *The Blue Eagles*, *The Island That Wasn't*, and *The River Without An End*. I know Tarketi, your guide, and Mahomet, the man who always lied to you . . .'

'Please, please, Miss Roubin,' he protested, and she saw that he was laughing. 'You've completely convinced me. You really have read my books.'

She sank back on her elbows, feeling suddenly exhausted and aware that she had been almost rude to him. 'I'm sorry, Mr. Harvey,' she said nervously. 'It was just that when—when you suggested I might be lying . . .'

His face was grave. 'I think I should apologize, but I didn't mean to accuse you. It's simply that I've got so used to people

39

pretending that they have read my books that I'm afraid I'm a little sceptical.'

'Miss Woubin! Miss Woubin!' Deborah was racing towards them, shouting. Then she flung herself on the ground between them, smiling at them both. 'You're both my fwiends, so you must be fwiends. Isn't that wight?' she asked eagerly.

Lauren and Roland Harvey exchanged a significant smile.

'Of course we must be friends, poppet,' Lauren said, but it all seemed unreal—like an impossible dream.

'Miss Roubin and I are already good friends,' Roland Harvey said quietly. 'She has read my books and, I hope, enjoyed them.'

'Oh, I did,' Lauren said earnestly. 'They opened up a new world to me.'

'A new world?' he asked, turning to her. Deborah was leaning against him, sorting out the shells she had gathered.

Lauren felt herself colouring. 'I mean . . . it made me see what sort of an exciting world it can be. My life is so very ordinary—so unadventurous. Yours is so different. It reminds me of my father's life, helps me understand him better.'

'Your father's life?'

She hesitated. Was she boring him? Was he just being polite?

Deborah looked up, her eyes bright with interest.

'Is your father an explorer, Miss Woubin?'

Lauren smiled at her. 'No, poppet, but he is—or was—a deep sea diver. He used to go down deep into the sea, Deborah, and find all sorts of treasures.'

'Chests of gold?' Deborah asked eagerly.

Lauren laughed. 'Well, not exactly, but old coins, old bits of pottery that had been buried in the sea for hundreds of years . .'

'He has retired?' Roland Harvey asked quietly.

Lauren looked at him. 'Yes. He got the bends very badly and it affected his heart, so he had no choice. He hates it. I expect you would.'

Roland Harvey nodded. 'I certainly would. What does he do with himself all day?'

'Oh, he fishes, and he's a keen gardener; then he lectures at the local schools—oh, and he runs the Sea Scouts and he trains deep sea divers occasionally.'

'In other words, he sublimates his needs,' Roland Harvey said thoughtfully. 'A wise and clever man. Your mother must have been glad when he had to retire.'

Lauren looked thoughtful. 'I suppose she was in a way, but it didn't strike me at the time. I do remember that when Dad came home he always got a fine welcome, but I know she was worried, too, when he had to retire. I remember her saying that he had always been free and she didn't know how he

41

would manage.'

'Your mother sounds a most unusual woman, Miss Roubin,' Roland Harvey said slowly. 'Didn't she hate him diving, want him to stop?' The question was put casually, but Lauren sensed a purpose behind the question. 'Wasn't she alarmed for his safety?'

Lauren frowned as she tried to remember. 'I sup-pose she must have been, but she never told us children, though we always knew when Dad was on a dangerous job.'

'How did you know?' Roland Harvey asked quietly.

Lauren half-closed her eyes, remembering . . . Those days when she lived at home, going to the local convent school and loving her ballet lessons. That was before she joined the Barton School of Ballet and went to live in London. 'I remember that she would have a thorough spring-cleaning of the house. We used to moan like mad because all our cupboards and drawers had to be turned out, and . . . and she used to hum a lot. That was a sure sign. It was sometimes as if she couldn't stop.'

'You weren't afraid for your father?'

Startled, Lauren looked at the big, handsome man by her side. 'Oh no! You see, to us Dad was someone very special. He was so tall and so strong and he knew everything. We were all sure that nothing could hurt him. We used to get impatient with Mummy and say she fussed. I can understand better now.'

Roland Harvey was tracing something in the white sand with his finger. 'I have a theory that men who live dangerously should never marry,' he said slowly.

Lauren caught her breath. Was this what it had all been leading up to? She glanced at the child, but Deborah was engrossed in examining and sorting her shells, her face absorbed.

'Don't you think,' Lauren began nervously, 'that the choice should be made by the woman? I mean, if you love someone very much, you obviously won't expect him to give up his life's work just because . . . because you're afraid for him.'

With a quick movement, Roland Harvey took off his dark glasses and looked at her. 'Wouldn't you? Yes, *you*, Miss Roubin.' His voice was hard. 'It's so easy to talk, but if you loved a man who lived dangerously, wouldn't you expect him to give it up and settle down to a safe existence in some dull suburb?'

Her hand flew nervously to her throat at the unexpected attack. 'I've never thought about it. I—I think if I loved him . . . enough to want to marry him, I would want him to be happy.'

He stared at her, his strange blue-grey eyes suddenly cold and accusing. He put on his glasses and turned away.

'It's so easy to talk, but I don't suppose you even know what it means to love someone.

You're probably like all women—selfish, possessive, demanding.' His voice was bitter, and as he spoke he was on his feet with a quick easy movement. His hand lightly ruffled Deborah's hair as she stared up at him. 'Take care of yourself, Deborah,' he said gently. 'I'll see you again very soon.' Then he gave a funny little bow to Lauren. 'Doubtless we shall meet again, Miss Roubin, as we share a mutual friend. It has been an interesting conversation, but think over what I've just said and I think you'll find that you would be no different from any other woman.' He lifted his hand in salute and walked away.

Lauren lay back on the sand, resting on one elbow, and watched his effortless rapid strides cover the blinding white sand. What a strange conversation it had become, and why was he so bitter? How odd that they should have so quickly reached the stage of discussing love and marriage.

Was he right? If she loved a man, would she want to tie him down to a safe job? Could she bear calmly to kiss him goodbye as if he were going to a safe desk in an office, but knowing in truth that he might never return? Could she be calm and accept his daily battle with death? Could she be as strong as her mother had been and leave him free to do what he liked?

'He is nice, isn't he, Miss Woubin?' Deborah said. She smiled at Lauren and there was a happy, proud note in her voice. 'He's

44

going to be my new daddy.'

Lauren stared at the freckled, sandy-haired child who looked so sure of herself. 'Your new daddy?' she echoed.

Deborah nodded. She gave a sudden impish grin. 'Swear 'cross your heart not to tell anyone, Miss Woubin. Mummy told me it was still a secwet.'

'A secret?' She seemed only able to echo Deborah's words. The most absurd sort of desolation filled her.

Deborah nodded violently. 'M'm . . . they don't want anyone to know yet, not even me.' She grinned again. 'Mummy wants him to settle down and stop his gadding about.' The words sounded strange on the young lips.

Lauren looked at her watch. 'Goodness, darling, you'll be late for lunch. I'll take you back.'

Deborah dusted the sand off her hands and stood up, giving an angelic smile. 'Please don't hover, Miss Woubin. I know my way and I'm quite used to looking after me.' She dusted the sand off her small body. 'I'll see you later?' she asked wistfully.

Lauren hesitated for a moment. 'I'll be here until three o'clock, but then I'll have to go,' she said.

Deborah beamed. 'I'll see you as soon as I've had my rest,' she promised, and darted off, her small legs flying across the sand.

Left alone, Lauren closed her eyes. There

45

were things she must think about—a decision she must make.

But she knew that already she had made it. Now she must get Nick to agree. Somehow she must make him understand.

Roland Harvey was not the stern tyrant they had imagined, or that Miss Hunter had implied. He was sympathetic and tolerant. He would understand why they had arranged for her to take Natalie's place. It would be a thousand times better to tell him the truth than to let him find out.

That he would never forgive.

## CHAPTER THREE

That afternoon, after they had finished practising their dances, Lauren told Nick that she had to see him.

'It's important,' she told him urgently, 'and we must be alone.'

He looked amused, but suggested they went up to her room.

'Don't forget your hair,' he warned her.

'I've ten minutes,' she said, looking anxiously at her watch. Somehow she must make Nick understand.

'Go ahead, cut the cackle and get down to business,' he said, laughing at her, and sitting in an armchair sideways, his legs dangling over

46

the arm, and lighting a cigarette.

She wished she had the gift of words for, as she told Nick everything, she saw that he was not convinced at all.

She started from the beginning—where Deborah had recognized her and so she had met Mrs. Lindstrom, who also recognized her. How later, on the sands, Roland Harvey had come along with Deborah.

As she spoke, she watched two deep lines between Nick's eyebrows deepen, but he remained silent until she had finished.

'Nick, he was so nice, so friendly and kind. I'm sure he would understand if we explained everything to him. He isn't nearly as cold and stern as I thought, but if he found out that we had lied . . .' She gave a little shiver as she stood there, hands clasped tightly, her eyes pleading, her voice desperate. 'I hate to think what he'd say. We must tell him the truth, Nick.'

He leaned forward and stubbed out his cigarette with a quick impatient movement. His head was framed by the view through the open windows. The blue sky, the distant shimmering water, voices and laughter drifted in on the wind that was so gentle it barely moved the graceful fronds of the palm trees. It was a very hot day, but suddenly, to Lauren, the room seemed icily cold as Nick looked at her.

'Are you quite mad, Lauren?' he asked

47

sharply. 'Simply because you've seen this man in a good mood for an hour or so, you imagine you can judge him. Miss Hunter must know him better than you do, and she said it was out of the question to expect him to understand.'

'But, Nick, he—' Lauren tried to speak.

Nick was on his feet. She had never seen him so angry before. 'You would really let me run the risk of losing this job, anger Miss Cartwright and perhaps ruin my future and Natalie's? All because of a childish hunch you've got that Mr. Roland Harvey would *understand*?' His eyes were hard. 'Come off it, Lauren. How naive can a girl be? In addition, what about Miss Hunter? It might make him so mad that she might lose her job, too. Is that a way to repay her? After all, she has taken a risk in keeping us on.'

'But, Nick, I'm sure she's quite wrong and he'd understand,' Lauren said desperately.

'For Pete's sake, stop acting like a silly little fool,' Nick said crossly. 'We'd find ourselves on the next plane to England and there would be a scathing note in the post for Miss Cartwright.' He seemed to tower above her, he was so angry. 'Look, let's have no more of this nonsense, Lauren. I know what I'm doing, and what I say goes. Unfortunately you've got us in this mess, so you must try and get us out of it. You must just keep out of the way and not run into the Lindstroms again.' He strode furiously to the door, opened it and slammed

48

it behind him.

Lauren stood still in the centre of the room. It was the nearest approach she had ever had to a quarrel with Nick. She felt exhausted and a little scared. Then she saw the time—that wretched hairdresser!

Later, as she lay in the warm fragrant bath and could hear voices in the corridor as people walked along it, she wondered if Nick was right and she was wrong. After all, he was much more experienced than she was, he had danced in many hotels, and, as he had said, surely Miss Hunter should know Roland Harvey better than she did?

Yet she still felt sure that they were wrong about Roland Harvey. He was not the difficult tyrant they made him out to be. A strong man, he would not stoop to such pettiness, she felt sure. But had she the right to go on fighting Nick about this? His whole future might be at stake.

Mentally she shook herself and relaxed in the warm water. How lovely a hot bath could be! She would really rather not risk Mr. Harvey's wrath in case it meant leaving here . . . this fairyland was something a girl dreamed about but could never hope would come true. Roland Harvey's friendliness had been heady, and maybe she was wrong and Nick was right. He was such an exciting, impressive sort of man that it was difficult not to feel thrilled because he had been so kind.

Drying herself on the large, luxuriously soft towel, she went on wondering and more and more, she began to think that Nick could be right and she might be wrong. After all, Deborah had been with them, and she had heard that woman at the lecture say that Roland Harvey loved children, especially little girls, and so mightn't that mean that when he was with them he would be in a gentle mood? Mightn't this vanish when Deborah wasn't there? Was it worth risking everything?

Dressing slowly for the evening with Claudia's aid, she turned and twisted before the mirror, amazed, as always, with what she saw. What a mind Nick had—what imagination! Tonight she wore a gown with a skirt made of layers of soft net, ranging from palest rose to deepest crimson. The tight strapless bodice was of softest green silk, pleated and supposed to be the calyx of the flower, Nick had said. Her hair was pale green, and he had told her to use green eye-shadow and a strange-coloured powder and lipstick. But strange as it was, the effect was wonderful, and it would look even more lovely in the concentrated glare of the spotlights.

Nick was a wonderful man. Miss Cartwright had told her that Nick did the choreography of the dance and designed the frocks Natalie should wear.

Tonight the theme of the dances was to be gaiety, youth, joyousness, the sweet perfume of a young summer . . . As she looked at herself, she thought how far removed from gaiety she felt. She hated quarrelling with anyone and it might make Nick difficult, moody, and frightening to dance with. Would he still be angry?

Her fears vanished when he came to fetch her and his hands were warm and gentle on her bare shoulders as she looked up at him nervously.

'Don't look like that, honey child,' he said quietly. 'I'm sorry I let off steam like that, but you had me really frightened for a while. You see, you're such a good little kid and you always think the best of everyone, but by the time you're my age, you'll be more sceptical. I'm sure Roland Harvey wouldn't waste time listening to my hard luck story—he would simply see that his orders had been flouted, and that would be that.' He paused and looked anxiously into her face. 'You do see, don't you?'

She felt ashamed that she had upset him so much.

'Of course, Nick. I've been thinking about it, and you're quite right.' She smiled at him. 'Besides, you're the boss.'

'There's my girl!' he said, and put his arm round her shoulders and hugged her. 'Come along. I have a feeling that tonight we're going to dance as we've never danced before.'

Nick must be psychic, Lauren thought, as

the evening slowly passed. It was a wonderful evening in every way. Now she felt completely relaxed, content to accept Nick's ruling that the secret must be kept. Her fear of being sent away from this island paradise had been lifted. As the music began, the butterflies inside her vanished and she was laughing up at Nick happily as he led her on to the floor, lightly swinging her hand. Everything was right the music perfect, their minds attuned, the atmosphere very friendly. The audience seemed to catch the true meaning of the dances, and a wave of enthusiasm swept them at the end of the dances and Nick and Lauren took more bows than they had done on the night before.

Miss Hunter joined them as they were finishing their dinner. She swept majestically into the small room, her head held arrogantly high; elegant in a sheath frock of gold lamé, her dark silky hair swept up into a knot on top of her head, pinned there by a large barbaric-looking gold pin.

'You did very well tonight,' she said in her dry toneless voice. 'But I think when you have finished eating, you must mix with the guests. Several of the gentlemen have expressed a wish to meet . . . Natalie.' Her eyes were cold as she looked at the startled girl. Then she turned to Nick. 'I trust that she knows how to handle any situation that might arise? With diplomacy? That absurd fantasy of

52

sophistication behind which she hides doesn't deceive me. She is and she behaves like a country girl . . .' Miss Hunter ignored Lauren's suddenly red cheeks, her quick protest, and her thin mouth relaxed into a smile. 'I'm aware that you're going to keep an eye on her, Nick, but please do try and talk some sense into her as well. You must *both* mix with the guests— it's part of the contract.'

'As you say, Miss Hunter,' Nick said quietly.

At the door, Miss Hunter turned, her eyes flicking over Nick's handsome face, his dark thoughtful eyes, his tall lean body. 'I would like to see you in my office at ten o'clock tomorrow morning, Nick,' she said curtly.

'As you say, Miss Hunter,' Nick said again, this time smiling a little.

As the door closed, he turned to the silent Lauren.

'Don't let that—that witch upset you, honey child. She just loves being nasty. Never let her see that she's hurt you. I know you can cope all right. Just stay away from deserted moonlit verandas, and if anyone gets a bit amorous, remind him that you're in love with your husband and that he's a very jealous man!'

They were laughing together as they went back to the ballroom.

Much later that night, as she lay in bed, Lauren thought how fortunate it was that she was with a man like Nick; a man who seemed to understand and sympathize as well, a man who gave her confidence and courage. It had been a lovely evening. The men she had danced with had been extremely nice, she had been toasted, complimented, teased, and had loved it all. This was how it must feel to be a beauty queen, she thought happily. She loved the V.I.P. treatment she had received. A few men had tried to make her drink alcohol and then she had laughingly parried, had said she only liked tomato juice, and they had finally accepted her word. Nick had told her that he was proud of her and she had thoroughly enjoyed it all.

There had been a thread of fear running through it all, of course—the fear lest she see Roland Harvey and he ask her for a dance. How, if that happened, could she prevent him from recognizing her? She must practise a new voice, deeper, huskier, perhaps, in case of such an event. But she had not seen him the whole time, nor had she seen Mrs. Lindstrom.

Were they, perhaps, having a little intimate dinner alone in Mr. Harvey's suite? Perhaps planning their future? Was Roland Harvey in love with Leila Lindstrom? It was likely—for she had great beauty and elegance. At the same time, it was hard to imagine Roland Harvey being in love with her . . . in love with anyone for that matter.

Nick's last words that night had been: 'Stay away from the Lindstrom kid, Lauren, and try not to meet Roland Harvey.'

It would not be easy. In the morning, Lauren awoke early and slipped away to the family lagoon while most of the families were still at breakfast. Deliberately she walked away from Deborah's pointed rock and went to the far side of the lagoon, feeling she was being unkind to Deborah, whose fault it was not, but maybe Nick was right and this was the best way. She found a solitary palm that threw welcome shade on the hot white sand. Close by was a tiny pool, fringed with small coloured stones. She spread her towel and began to write a letter to her family. There was so much to tell them and the day was deliciously hot so that the temptation to relax and close her eyes, drifting into dreams, was almost overwhelming, but she fought it. She told them about the wonderful hotel, about the beauty of the island, about Deborah, about the famous Roland Harvey . . . but she did not tell them that she was supposed to be Natalie Natal and that they had not told Roland Harvey the truth. She knew what her parents would have said—they would have said the truth must always be told, and although she felt they were right, she had to do what Nick said. After all, but for Nick, she would not have been here.

Deborah found her at last, falling on to her with cries of triumph. 'I looked and I looked and I looked,' she said eagerly. 'Mummy said I could swim if I found you.' She plumped herself down on the hot sand by Lauren's side, beaming at her.

Lauren had to smile. It looked as if she was going to be useful to Mrs. Lindstrom! Not that she minded—she loved Deborah, but it meant that Roland Harvey might be involved as well and Nick would be mad with her. There was nothing to be done at the moment, though, so she relaxed and enjoyed herself with Deborah. They found the little pool was deep enough for the child to try to swim properly in it, and they were in and out of the water the whole time, laughing, enjoying it together. At lunch time Deborah trotted off dutifully, and very soon Lauren followed her example and got a cold lunch with a wonderful salad from the conveniently handy little buffet set up near the beach. Then she went back to her palm tree and little pool and tried to write some more of her letter. The letter went slowly, for there was so much beauty to look at—the expanse of blue water, the whiteness of the sand, the huge palm trees. It was all so wonderful, like a Technicolor film. It didn't seem possible that this could be happening to her ...

Shadows fell across her writing pad and she looked up, expecting to see Deborah. To her dismay—but inward joy—she saw that Roland Harvey was holding Deborah's hand and gazing down at Lauren as she sat on the sands.

'Shall we disturb you?' he asked and, without waiting for a reply, sat down by her side.

Hastily she thrust her letter away, her cheeks warm as she wondered what he would say if he could read the nice things she had said about him to her mother. 'I was only writing home,' she said, hastily zipping the writing case together.

He smiled. 'Good girl. Deborah and I are going swimming. Care to join us?'

'Miss Woubin is teaching me to swim,' Deborah said, dancing round them, her feet sending up little spatters of sand. 'I love Miss Woubin and Miss Woubin loves me.'

Roland Harvey smiled at her. 'I'm not surprised . . . in either case.' He turned to Lauren. 'You're fond of children, Miss Roubin?' His voice was kind but impersonal.

Lauren rested her weight on her hands, leaning back, feeling her shoulder-length hair swinging gently. 'Yes, I am. I teach children ballet, you know, Mr. Harvey.'

He was staring at her, his dark glasses hiding his expression. 'So I understand, Miss Roubin. Deborah enjoys her lessons.'

She wondered why he was staring at her so intently, and had a moment of panic as she wondered if she had washed all the green rinse out of her hair. But it seemed as though it must be all right, for they went on to talk about dancing, and how it gave Deborah self-confidence, and then he persuaded Deborah to stop dancing around them, for she was showing off a little to him, and asked her to

57

arrange her precious shells into a pattern.

'No, tell me a stowy,' Deborah insisted, curling up by his side.

Roland Harvey smiled a little apologetically at Lauren.

'We'll get no peace if I don't,' he murmured.

He told Deborah that when he was a little boy, his parents had gone to a faraway land where children could not live, and so he had lived with his uncle.

'Uncle Horace was very kind to me,' he said thoughtfully, 'and I've often realized since that I didn't appreciate all he did for me. I'm afraid children are often selfish without realizing it . . .' He talked of his childhood in Cornwall, of his interest in stories about smugglers. 'I think I always was a rebel,' he said with a half smile. 'I decided there and then that when I was a man I would be an explorer. All my work at school and at university was headed in that direction, and as soon as I could, I went off on different expeditions. I was rarely at home. I'm afraid I never thought that my uncle might need me. It must have been all of eight years since I last saw him,' he said ruefully, 'when I heard he was dead. Uncle Horace had a big heart—he left me all his money and this hotel.'

Deborah was leaning against him, her eyes drowsy and her cheeks flushed. 'Is that why you're so very wich?' she asked sleepily.

Lauren watched the way the big man smiled at the child. How he loved her! How gentle and kind and loving he was with her. It seemed a strange trait in a hard, cold, brusque sort of man—but was Roland Harvey really all those things? Wasn't this relaxed man the real Roland Harvey? Wasn't his hardness a facade behind which he hid?

'Yes, darling, that's why I'm rich,' he said gently, and stared at the peaceful lagoon. They were at the most deserted end of the long beach and it was very quiet. 'That money means a lot to me,' he went on quietly, almost as if talking to himself. 'It means freedom—it opens the way for many expeditions. It means that now I can plan things my way and not the way of those who raise the money for us.' He turned to Lauren, and for a moment his face was that of an eager boy. 'It's like being given a fairy wand,' he said. 'Now so many of my dreams can come true.'

'You will sell the hotel?' she asked idly, fascinated by this new side of him.

She was startled when he frowned, for his whole face seemed to change, to become hard and suspicious. 'Who have you been talking to?' he demanded.

She was confused by his abrupt change of mood. 'No one—no one at all. It was just that—that you said now your dreams would come true, and I thought . . . well, I didn't think that running a hotel could be one of your dreams, so—so I thought you would be selling it and going off on another expedition.'

His face relaxed. 'I see. Of course you're right—in a way. That is what I would like to do, but one of the terms of the will was that I should run this hotel for a year before I made any decision to sell it or keep it. It seems that it was a dream come true for my uncle and he wanted to make it one of the finest hotels in the world.' His voice was dry. 'Apparently it wasn't . . . it isn't! Uncle Horace was getting old, and towards the end he left everything in the hands of his assistants. They were very efficient, but . . .' He frowned. Looking down, he saw that Deborah was asleep. He glanced at Lauren with a half-smile. 'I'm afraid I bored her. I expect I'm boring you, too?'

'Oh, no, you're not,' Lauren said eagerly. 'I'm most interested. I imagine it must be terribly hard to run a hotel successfully— especially one of this size and reputation— when you've had no experience at all.'

'It is,' Roland Harvey agreed. He eased the sleeping child, who lay against his arm, into a more comfortable position. 'You know,' he went on thoughtfully, 'the thing that puzzled me most here—and still does, for it hasn't changed—is the constant staff changes. I can't understand it, for I pay excellent salaries and I have a very good manager in Miss Hunter. She really does know her job. Yet there's something wrong here. Something seems to be festering, like a concealed sore.' He frowned. 'Do I sound absurdly fanciful? I just don't feel

60

the staff are happy.'

There was a pause. Lauren hunted wildly in her mind for an intelligent remark. In the end, she said unhappily: 'I wish I could help you, but I've never talked to any of the staff.'

Roland Harvey's face showed plainly his displeasure. Again! It was as if everything she said today was wrong.

'I certainly don't want you to discuss the position with the staff,' he said sharply. 'It's not your affair. You're here to enjoy yourself. I hope you are?'

'Oh, I am,' she said quickly. 'I think this is a lovely place.'

She wondered if he was surprised to think that she could afford a holiday like this. Perhaps he thought ballet teachers earned large salaries? If he only knew! He probably knew very little about how the world lived — he was probably so wrapped up in his precious expeditions. Or perhaps he didn't think about her at all.

They were silent for a while, and then Roland Harvey looked at his watch and at the angelic face of the sleeping child. 'She's a sweet child,' he said softly, 'but I gather from her mother that she's a bit of a handful.'

Lauren turned to him, her eyes flashing. 'What young child isn't?' she asked indignantly. 'When a child is meek and quiet, it's time to start worrying about her. Deborah is just a normal healthy child for her age, very

61

intelligent, rather un . . .' She stopped herself in time. She looked at him. 'I'm sure you were a handful at her age,' she finished lamely.

He put back his head and laughed. '*Touché!* I most certainly was.'

'You're very fond of children, and yet . . .' Lauren hesitated. 'Yet you've never married?' She found courage enough to say it, and then held her breath. Had she said the wrong thing again? Angered him?

But he did not seem annoyed. He merely smiled and asked: 'Have you never heard that hoary old cliché, "He travels fastest who travels alone"? Besides, I'm not an ordinary man. I mean, I don't lead a normal life. I don't think it's right to ask any woman to shoulder the burden of having to adapt herself to my way of living, for I certainly couldn't adapt myself.'

Or wouldn't, Lauren thought to herself. 'You've never been in love?' she asked, and wondered how she had the courage to say such a thing.

He laughed. 'Of course I've been in love. And out of it, pretty sharply, too, several times. There's nothing quite so disillusioning as finding that your adored angel has feet of clay. Look, Miss Roubin,' he went on, smiling at her, 'I'm thirty-six, is it likely I could live in a world of such beautiful women and walk unscathed? There was one girl, and I was very young—about twenty-five. She was . . . well,

62

very lovely. She told me frankly that I must give up my mad exploring and settle down in her father's firm. Guess what her father sold? Kitchen hardware. Saucepans and suchlike.' He laughed. 'I told her she didn't love me, and she burst into tears and said I didn't love her! *Impasse.* After that, I decided marriage was not for me. It's only when . . .' He looked down at the sleeping child and gently touched the freckles on her nose. 'It's only where children are concerned that sometimes I envy other men.'

'I think any woman who really loved you . . .' Lauren began.

Roland Harvey looked at her with what, she recognized with a shock, was pity. 'You said that before, Miss Roubin. I'm afraid you're too young to know what love is. You're little more than a child.'

'I'm twenty-one,' she said indignantly, tossing her head so that her ash-blonde curly hair swung with the movement.

He looked surprised. 'Are you really? I thought you were about seventeen.'

Was he teasing her? Did she really look only seventeen? Looking at him, she found herself believing him. Why, to him she was a child. A child to be treated kindly—in the way he treated Deborah.

But she was not a child. Nor did she want to be looked on as one—or treated as one. She was a woman.

But not to Roland Harvey. He had already forgotten her, and was looking at his watch worriedly. 'If Deborah wants to swim, I'll have to wake her up,' he said. 'I've an appointment.'

Tenderly and gently he awakened the child, giving her time to wake up properly, then he went swimming, into clear calm water with Deborah on his back, clutching his dark red hair, for once ruffled, her face ecstatic. He did not ask Lauren to join them, so she remained where she was, watching them, her face thoughtful and a little sad.

Surely she looked more than seventeen? Surely any man with eyes to see could tell that she was a woman, old enough and eager to be loved . . .

Suddenly she caught her breath. Watching the child and the big, handsome man romping like tortoises in the shallow water, she knew something . . .

And yet it was so crazy, so impossible, so incredible that she knew she must forget it at once.

She must not think about it again. Must wipe it out of her mind. It couldn't be, mustn't be true . . .

Telling herself this almost hysterically, she still knew the truth. This was something she could never forget. She was in love with Roland Harvey.

How long she lay there on the sands, still and scared, she did not know. This was something too big for her to handle. She couldn't be so foolish. It was asking for trouble, for pain, sorrow, heartache. Then something made her look at her watch and she leapt to her feet in dismay. She had less than five minutes in which to get back to the hotel, change into a frock and join Nick.

She turned to run, giving one last look towards the lagoon, and saw that Roland Harvey was on his feet, staring after her, and that Deborah was jumping up and down by his side, obviously telling him something. Was she saying that Miss Woubin was like Cindewella, that she had to go at three o'clock? Would that make him wonder? Make him suspicious? Yet why should it? He probably forgot all about her the instant he left her side. To Roland, she was just an unsophisticated, rather silly young girl. That was how he saw her. And that was something she must remember . . .

She was running towards the hotel when Mrs. Lindstrom stopped her. As usual immaculate, she wore a blue sun-frock.

'Miss Roubin,' she said sharply, 'what have you done with Deborah?'

Somehow Lauren managed to move past her, saying: 'Sorry, but I'm late, Mrs. Lindstrom. Deborah is quite all right. I left her with Mr. Harvey.'

'You left her with—?' Mrs. Lindstrom began, but Lauren did not wait to hear any more. There was a strange look on Mrs.

Lindstrom's face, but Lauren could only think of one thing—that Nick would be waiting for her and she didn't want to make him angry. And whatever happened, she knew, she must never let Nick guess her secret. If he knew that she was in love with Roland Harvey—or thought she was, as he would surely say—he would do his best to make it impossible for her to see Roland Harvey again.

## CHAPTER FOUR

It was to be a whole week before Lauren saw Deborah again. At first it did not worry her very much, for the days slipped by so easily that she was hardly aware of the passage of time. Each day she spent on the hot white sands and she had discovered a discreet pathway that wound in and out through many flowering bushes and which allowed her to reach the sands without using the wide road where most people walked. She acquired the habit of slipping out of the hotel very early every morning and going along this pathway to the part of the beach she preferred, by the solitary palm tree and the little pool. As very few hotel guests walked as far along the sands as that, she had it almost entirely to herself.

Lying there contentedly in the sunshine, writing letters or just dreaming, she did not really miss Deborah. Sometimes when she thought of the child, she wondered where she was, but it did not actively worry her until the seventh day. She kept telling herself that it was really all for the best. If Deborah came to see her, there was every chance that Roland Harvey would too, and although one half of her longed to see him, the other, saner, more sensible half agreed that it was best for him to stay away.

Her love was doomed to be only a source of pain to her. All the dreaming in the world could not make her think otherwise. Even if Roland Harvey saw her as a woman—a woman ready for love—there would still be no hope for her. He was determined not to marry. Hadn't he told her so? And despite Deborah's wide-eyed certainty that he was to be her new father, Lauren thought it extremely doubtful. Somehow she could not see him as the lovely Leila Lindstrom's husband. Somehow she could not see him as anyone's husband.

The days seemed to fly by—living to a routine as she did ensured that. There were fresh dances to be practised every afternoon, then the hairdresser to visit as he colour-rinsed and twisted her hair into the strangest of colours and shapes, and then came the long time she took to bath, dress and make up in accordance with Nick's instructions. Next would come the ever-increasing thrill of waiting for the drums to roll, and then it was time to give Nick her hand and let him lead her out on to the floor, and everything else would be forgotten in the excitement and wonder of the dance and the ever-satisfying roar of applause.

She had grown used to mingling with the guests afterwards, dancing with them, laughing with them, refusing the champagne that was always offered to her, bearing their teasing good-humouredly when she insisted on having tomato juice.

She loved her beautiful gowns, each one so different—the gracious white satin gown, designed like a lily; the pale lilac gown that was just a froth of organdie with an ostrich feather bodice; the dramatic scarlet sheath with the hidden fullness of skirt; the cream satin crinoline with the great loops of scarlet roses on the skirt. Each gown was designed for a special series of dances, for a theme; each evening there was a different motif—sometimes happiness, sometimes tragedy. It was more than mere dancing; Nick was an artist. It was fun to learn the different dances—to practise the verve and abandon of the Spanish dance, the subtle nuances of the Japanese, the gaiety of the Irish, the formality and precision of the Scottish, and then there was always the sheer beauty of straight ballroom dancing. She loved the graceful beauty of the waltz, the dignity of the slow fox-trot, the tangos that Nick danced with such grace and arrogance. In fact, had she been asked which was her favourite dance, she would have found it hard to decide. She loved them all.

Of course always there was the fear that one day she would meet Roland Harvey face to face, that he would ask her for a dance, recognize her and . . .

Whenever she got to this stage, her thoughts balked. What would he do, say? Fortunately he rarely appeared in the ballroom in the evenings; even when he dined there, he usually vanished soon afterwards. Luckily, too, she had not come in contact with Mrs. Lindstrom, although Nick was sure that Leila Lindstrom would not recognize the young unsophisticated Lauren in the beautiful, glamorous Natalie Natal.

Not that seeing Roland Harvey prevented Lauren from thinking about him. As she lay on the warm sands, eyes shut, hidden by the dark glasses, she would try to analyse her feelings if she were his wife . . . would she gladly see him go off on an expedition down the dangerous Amazon? Or would she cling to him and tearfully beg him not to go? Wouldn't she be like any other woman—try to persuade him to seek a safe job, a job from which he came home each night, a job in which she could share his interests, be close to him? How had her mother managed and remained so serene?

It was on the seventh day that she began to

worry about Deborah. Could Mrs. Lindstrom have left the hotel?

There was an English girl in charge of the linen on Lauren's floor—a pretty girl called Rene Thompson, who was normally a nurse but who had taken this job, she said, because she was tired of English winters. Tall, thin, with straight dark hair falling over one eye, she knew Lauren only as Lauren, never being around when Lauren turned into Natalie, with her exotic make-up and extravagant costumes. One morning, hurrying down to the beach, Lauren stopped by the linen-room where Rene Thompson was checking the bed linen and towels with the African maids.

'Want something?' Rene asked with a friendly smile.

'In a way,' Lauren said. 'I wondered if you had seen little Deborah Lindstrom about. I haven't seen either the child or her mother for a week. I was wondering if they had left, or if the child was ill.'

She wondered why Rene smiled strangely and said: 'No, she's not ill. Just being kept on ice.'

'On ice?' Lauren said, puzzled.

Rene said something to the maids and then strolled down the corridor with Lauren. She looked very pretty and competent in her lilac nylon overall.

'Surely you know,' Rene said in a low confidential voice, 'that Mrs. Lindstrom is trying to hook the boss and is using the child as bait? We get it on the local grapevine. It seems that the bait was wandering away from Mama and enticing the boss to another lady.' Her eyes were significantly amused as she looked meaningly at Lauren. 'How did you work it, you clever girl?' she asked.

Lauren's cheeks were hot. 'I didn't work it!' she exclaimed.

She was startled and shocked to think of the gossip that was apparently going round the hotel. And she had thought no one would notice her!

Rene put her finger on the side of her nose and smiled.

'You're too modest, Miss Roubin. You're something of a mystery, too. Tell me, how come you're such a nice, innocent-looking little girl mornings and then in the middle of the afternoon and evening you become the exotic, fabulous Natalie Natal?'

Dismayed, Lauren faced her. 'Does everyone know?' she asked.

Rene Thompson chuckled. 'But of course. You haven't a hope of hiding anything from the grapevine here—you were mad to think so.'

Lauren's mouth was dry. 'Mr. Harvey . . .' she began.

'Obviously doesn't know,' Rene Thompson supplied the words. 'I suppose you had to pay through the nose to keep the Hunter's ugly

71

mouth shut?'

Startled, Lauren stared at her. 'I don't know ... I mean, Nick handled it all ...'

'I bet he had to,' Rene said. 'Just like she takes a slice off our salaries,' she added bitterly.

Lauren stared at her in amazement. 'Does she? Surely she can't do that?'

'Can't she? She most certainly does. If you cavil about it, you get the sack. Oh, very politely and most reasonably. There's always a perfectly legitimate reason why you have to leave, but leave you do, and quick. Unless you're prepared to pay Hunter a slice—and believe me, it's a pretty generous one.'

'I don't get paid,' Lauren said. 'I'm working for the Cartwright School of Dancing, so—'

'But I bet your handsome Nick earns something on the side from dancing lessons. I bet she gets a slice out of that,' Rene Thompson said. Suddenly she was laughing. 'Don't look so stricken. It isn't the end of the world. But it's the reason why the staff keeps changing. Some of us can take it for so long, and then we rebel against the injustice of it. Still, you've nothing to moan about—a nice easy job, a gorgeous brute of a man to dance with, and Roland Harvey himself sneaking off to meet you on the sands. You're doing pretty well for yourself.'

'He didn't sneak off,' Lauren said indignantly.

72

Rene was laughing. 'Whatever he did, we all admire you for it but don't count on it getting you far. You haven't a hope, for you're far too nice a girl. In this battle for a man, no holds are barred.'

Lauren was beginning to wish she had never stopped to talk to Rene Thompson. 'I don't understand,' she said stiffly.

Rene stared at her. 'Really? Surely you know that the poor man is already being tussled over by Mrs. Leila Lindstrom and by the Hunter herself?'

'Miss Hunter?' Lauren gasped.

They were standing in a quiet angle of the corridors; they could see down both corridors so that there was no danger of being overheard. Lauren felt dazed. Was Miss Hunter so greedy and unprincipled? No wonder the staff was constantly changing. What would Roland Harvey say if he knew? What would he think of his wonderful, efficient Miss Hunter whom he trusted so implicitly?

'Sure, why not?' Rene Thompson was saying. 'She nearly caught old Horace Harvey. Maybe she'd have succeeded if he hadn't had that stroke. She was pretty mad, and we all suffered when she heard that he had left her nothing. She was always sucking up to him and being oh, so charming!'

Lauren felt suddenly sick. 'You hate her, don't you?' she said.

Rene tossed her hair back. 'Sure I hate her, and with good cause. I need every penny I can earn. I don't tell people as a rule, but I was in hospital sick for a long time, and now my mother is ill. I want to save enough to get her out of England and give her a good rest, and when I have to hand over some of my hard-earned money to that—that vulture . . . well, I'm afraid I see red. Anyhow, the Hunter wants this hotel for her own, and she means to get it, by fair means or foul. The betting is pretty even on the two of them, and now you've come along to throw a spanner in the works. Good for you!' Rene smiled at her.

'But . . . but I'm not in it,' Lauren said, and saw that Rene did not believe her. 'He just sees me as a child, a child like Deborah. That reminds me, what did you mean about Deborah being kept on ice?'

Rene chuckled. 'Just that Mrs. Lindstrom won't allow the child to wander about the beach any more. Mornings she's put in the nursery with the other unwanted kids, afternoons Mrs. Lindstrom hopefully takes her on the beach, but so far Mr. Harvey has kept away. Mrs. Lindstrom must be mad with him and with you. Watch out for her, these women can be dangerous. Well, so long, I'd better get back to my job. Good hunting!' Rene said, touching Lauren lightly on the arm. 'But don't count on winning,' she said with a laugh as she turned away.

Lauren hurried to the beach and her favourite place. She felt shocked and somehow as if she needed a bath. There had been such venom in Rene Thompson's voice, and yet she could sympathize with her. How maddening it must be to have Miss Hunter take part of your money. It was also a shock to realize that the staff knew that she was both Natalie Natal and Lauren Roubin. Somehow she had not thought of there being gossip in an hotel. Had Nick? Perhaps he had felt sure that no one would betray a fellow employee.

But that the gossip should be that she was trying to trap Roland Harvey! It made her squirm and want to run and hide.

Yet was it really a terrible thing to try to make a man love you? Hadn't women often had to fight for the man they loved? Fight to win his love . . .

But it all made it sound so horribly sordid. When she loved a man, she wanted him to do the chasing. What sort of love was it when you had to—horrible expression—hook a man?

'Oh, there you are, Miss Roubin,' a voice said sharply.

Lauren opened her eyes and sat up, blinking up at Mrs. Lindstrom, who stood holding a very subdued Deborah by the hand.

'Where have you been hiding yourself all this time, Miss Roubin?' Mrs. Lindstrom asked—just as if Lauren had deliberately avoided them. 'Deborah has been most

75

unhappy.'

Lauren scrambled to her feet. The elegant Mrs. Lindstrom always made her feel at a disadvantage, so there was no reason to make it worse by being forced to stare up at her.

'I've been here every day,' she said. She smiled at Deborah, who smiled back, her eyes wary. 'I've missed Deborah, too.'

'Can I stay with Miss Woubin?' the child asked meekly.

Her mother inclined her head. 'Yes, if Miss Roubin doesn't object. I'll see you later.' She walked off, hardly bothering to look at Lauren, who thought how slim and elegant she was in her white swimsuit, and how very rude she could be.

'Oh, Miss Woubin, I've missed you so,' Deborah said, hugging her warmly. 'I hate that nursery.' Her voice was trembling. 'They're all such babies, and they cry and fight and . . .'

Lauren held Deborah's small sticky hand tightly. 'I know, poppet,' she said sympathetically. 'Now what about a swimming lesson?'

Deborah's eyes began to shine. 'I've got my swimsuit on under this,' she said eagerly, trying to undo the knot at the back of her sun-suit.

'Let me,' Lauren said, and then slipped out of her shorts.

They swam and frolicked in the warm water and then sat talking on the sands until it was time for Deborah to trot off to lunch.

'You will be here this afternoon, Miss Woubin?' she asked wistfully.

'Of course, but I have to go just before three o'clock,' Lauren said.

She watched the small girl walk away over the blinding white sand, and then she leant back on her arms, gazing at the sea thoughtfully. Now why had Mrs. Lindstrom suddenly released her child from bondage and allowed her to return to Lauren? Mrs. Lindstrom must have a reason for it.

Lauren stopped her thoughts abruptly. How catty she was getting! After all, what sort of plan could Mrs. Lindstrom have and what part could she want Lauren to play in it? It was nonsense.

Days drifted by and now Deborah always joined Lauren on the beach, and a little later they would be joined by Roland Harvey, who came to sit and talk with them under what Deborah called their own palm tree. Each day Lauren's depression deepened. Mr. Harvey was kind, too kind. He treated her exactly as he treated Deborah—with a gentle indulgence. Just as if the two girls were of the same age, instead of one being fifteen years older than the other!

One afternoon, they were lying on the warm sands, listening to the soft shushing of the water and the strange whispering noises a palm tree makes in a breeze, and Lauren looked surreptitiously at the man so intent on amusing Deborah. What a striking personality he had. He seemed to give off waves of strength.

She sighed, and Roland Harvey heard the sound and turned to her inquiringly. 'Why the big sigh?' he asked.

Her cheeks were hot. 'I was just thinking,' she told him.

'Homesick?'

'Not really.'

'I'm never homesick,' Deborah chimed in proudly. 'I'm always happy.'

The big man ruffled the child's hair affectionately.

'You're a happy little thing, Deborah. That's why I like you.'

Deborah's eyes were wide with excitement. 'You do like me?' she asked eagerly. 'My mummy told me to make you like me, and then . . .'

Lauren wondered who was the most embarrassed—she or Roland Harvey. It was the first time she had seen him discomfited.

'Of course I like you, Deborah,' he interrupted quickly. 'But where are those shells you promised me?'

Deborah's hand flew to her mouth, her eyes dismayed.

'I forgot them,' she said sadly. 'I'll get them now.'

There was a little silence as they watched her run off towards the lagoon. Homesick, he had said, Lauren thought miserably. What would he have said had she confessed the truth and said that she was lovesick—lovesick for him! How embarrassed he would be. Just as he had been just now when Deborah had so nearly betrayed a secret. Was there some understanding then between Roland Harvey and Leila Lindstrom? Yet Rene Thompson had suggested that Mr. Harvey and Miss Hunter might be involved in something more than a mere business association, that Miss Hunter hoped to marry him. Was Roland Harvey just being clever? Playing off the two women against one another? Yet it was so unlike him . . .

She leant forward, for he was staring at her, and her hair swung forward protectively. She was startled when he said quietly:

'You have very pretty hair.'

It was the last straw. She flung back her hair swiftly and stared at him, feeling her eyes sting. He had said the words in just the same sort of voice he used when he paid Deborah a compliment. To Roland Harvey, she was just a child. She fought back the angry words that trembled on her lips. If she was rude to him, she might never see him again alone. Even if these chance encounters hurt, she also got a lot of pleasure out of them. She was still sure that this was the real Roland Harvey, that the brusque impatient man the staff feared was a defence. But then why should a man like

79

Roland Harvey need such a defence?

'Deborah seems to have found plenty of shells,' Lauren said, her voice stiff, as they watched the small girl come towards them. Something made her add: 'She loves you very much, Mr. Harvey.'

'I love her, too,' the big man said very quietly. 'You know, I had a young sister, and she died, in a car crash. I don't think I shall ever forget that day. I was very young, but I can remember my mother asking my father not to drive so fast. I can still hear his laughter, he called her a scaredy-cat . . . the expression stuck in my mind for years afterwards. Well, we hit something pretty hard and I saw my small sister flying through the air, and then I blacked out. I was in hospital suffering from shock for some time and both my parents were injured, but it was only Carol who died. Some months later, my parents got a divorce, and that was when my uncle took me to live with him. I told Deborah my parents lived in a faraway land where children could not go . . . it was the truth in a way, for where there is divorce, it's the children who have no place to live. That's another reason why I'm so sorry for Deborah. Her parents are divorced and she inevitably suffers. She needs a father very badly.'

'Yes,' Lauren said, her mouth suddenly dry. So was he going to offer his services—as her father? Could Deborah be right? Could a man love a child so much that he be willing to give up his cherished freedom and marry her mother?

'Look! Look!' Deborah cried, as she reached them and flung herself down by their side. 'Look at my lovely shells.' She spread them out before her.

Lauren managed to say the right things, but her thoughts were far away. Suddenly she was very conscious of the big man by her side. Why had he talked so frankly to her? His deep voice had not sounded as it usually did—crisp, issuing orders. He had spoken gently, thoughtfully . . .

As if to a child. It was the voice he used when talking to Deborah.

She saw the time on her watch and was shocked. How the hours flew by! 'I must go or I'll be late,' she said, gathering up her beach bag, putting the writing case and sunburn lotion in it. Nick was rather moody these days and annoyed if she was a minute late.

'You must go?' Roland Harvey stared at her in surprise. 'It's—'

Deborah looked up with a beam.

'Poor Miss Woubin,' she said, 'she's like Cindewella, she always has to be in the hotel at three o'clock.'

Roland Harvey lifted his thick eyebrows quizzically.

'Someone important—your Prince Charming?' She knew that he was teasing her—in just the same way as he would tease Deborah—and the knowledge stung. Her cheeks were hot and she didn't answer.

'Have you a Pwince Charming, Miss Woubin?' Deborah asked eagerly. 'Can I be a bwidesmaid at your wedding?'

Lauren did not know what to say. She stood up, prepared for flight, trying to think of how to leave them politely.

But before she could say anything, Roland Harvey was laughing, ruffling Deborah's hair. 'Don't be foolish, Deborah child,' he said, and looked up at Lauren. 'Miss Roubin hasn't a Prince Charming yet —she's much too young.'

Clutching her towel and beach bag, Lauren gazed down at him miserably, glad of the knowledge that her dark glasses would hide the pain in her eyes.

'I'm not so young,' she began, and was shocked to hear that her voice was trembling. 'I'm twenty-one, and I'm a woman . . .'

She was conscious of the surprise on Roland Harvey's face. He had jerked off his dark glasses and she could see his strange blue-grey eyes. And suddenly it was more than Lauren could bear. This fine, handsome, fascinating man, and all he could see her as was a child. The words tumbled out of her mouth. 'And I'm ready for love,' she blurted.

She almost threw the words at him and then turned, stumbling a little as she ran over the hot sands, making for the narrow entrance to the pathway through the flowering shrubs that would lead her back to the hotel.

'Look where you're going,' a sharp voice cried.

Lifting her head, Lauren saw that she had nearly knocked Mrs. Lindstrom over in her mad blind rush.

'I'm sorry,' she gasped. 'I didn't see you.'

Mrs. Lindstrom was staring at her, her face suspicious.

'Now what have you been up to?' she demanded.

Lauren couldn't trust her own voice. She knew how near the tears were. She wondered what she looked like, with flushed cheeks and tearful eyes, but she did not care. She had been rude to Roland Harvey, that was all she knew.

## CHAPTER FIVE

That night they danced what was, to Lauren, a difficult dance. She was Autumn—in a chiffon gown of every shade from palest gold to deepest russet. Her hair was streaked to look like a falling leaf—and the motif was also carried on in the floating panels that hung from the shoulders of the gown and which she used, with their long flowing lines, to simulate the leaves as they fell. It was a dance that required concentration and good timing, and it had been extra difficult because of the inward turmoil of her thoughts. She found it impossible to forget how angrily and how rudely she had spoken to Roland Harvey—and, to make matters worse, she had brushed past Mrs. Lindstrom, ignoring her questions. You could be sure Mrs. Lindstrom would comment on it to Roland Harvey.

Afterwards, as she and Nick took their bows in the sudden brilliance of the lights, Lauren glanced round anxiously. Was Roland Harvey there that night? Would he recognize her?

Suddenly she felt Nick's fingers digging painfully into her arm and heard him saying softly but angrily in her ear: 'For Pete's sake, stop acting like a stork!'

Her face flamed with shame and hastily she lowered her foot to the ground. How could she have done such a thing, here in front of everyone?

Later, Nick scolded her. 'I thought you'd cured yourself of that childish habit,' he said crossly.

It was the last straw and her eyes filled with tears. 'I'm sorry. I—I didn't know I was doing it. I haven't done it for ages.'

'I know, that's why I was so surprised. It's out of keeping with Natalie Natal, that's all that worries me, Lauren. A schoolgirlish habit.' He paused, frowning a little. 'You tired? You must always tell me, honey child,' he went on. 'We could have done an easier dance, for we don't have to stick to a rigid schedule, you know. Are you worried about something?'

She took a deep breath. 'I was rude to Mr. Harvey today, Nick,' she began, and told him the whole story. 'If only he would stop seeing me as a small child of Deborah's age!'

Nick burst out laughing. 'You're a funny kid. It may be for the best in the long run, for now he'll think you're younger than ever.' He chuckled. 'It's only the very young who hate being called young. Natalie would have taken it as a compliment.

Lauren sighed. Even Nick didn't understand. It had nothing to do with her age, it was the fact that Roland Harvey saw her as a child and not as a woman.

Nick went on: 'If you did annoy him as you think, and he isn't a man to accept rudeness lightly, then maybe he'll keep away from you in future.' His voice changed abruptly. 'What sort of game is this you're playing, Lauren? Why don't you give him the brushoff—politely, of course? You know so much rests on his not finding out who you are.'

'I don't encourage him, and he isn't in the least interested in me,' Lauren said desperately. 'It's simply that Deborah happens to like me and—'

'Look, honey child,' Nick said worriedly. Had he seen the tears in her eyes? 'Slip off to bed. I'll make your excuses if necessary. You're not in the right spirit to dance with a lot of would-be wolves.'

'But what about Miss Hunter?' she asked.

Nick chuckled. 'She has a guest tonight. I heard her ordering a very special dinner for two to be served in her sitting-room. You run along. I'll cope.'

'Thanks a lot, Nick,' Lauren said gratefully, and hurried to the cool privacy of her room. It was a long time before she slept, for she kept thinking about that little scene on the sands. Just how rude had she been? Would Roland Harvey find it unforgivable of her?

In the morning when she awoke, she was filled with a deep depression, terrified at the thought of facing an angry Roland Harvey. Should she stay in her room? Wouldn't that be unfair to poor little Deborah?

So in the end, Lauren dressed carefully, choosing a honey-coloured swimsuit and matching shorts. She brushed her hair until it gleamed and she moved her head slowly, watching the silky bob swing, then in a sudden fit of anger with herself, twisted her hair up in a pony-tail and tied it with a green ribbon. How could she be so stupid as to dress up for a man who saw her only as a child!

Well, she would look like a child, if that was the way he wanted it! She rubbed the lipstick off her mouth and glared at her reflection. She looked ridiculously young now. Nearer fifteen than twenty-one.

She was shaking a little as she collected her dark glasses, writing case and beach bag. Not that he would notice she looked any different. Indeed, it was doubtful if he would even look her way if he was really angry.

She lay under what Deborah called 'their' palm tree, and had barely settled before Roland Harvey strode over the sands to join her.

He was alone. He was wearing a tropical, light-coloured suit and his red hair was well disciplined. His face was grave.

'May I join you, Miss Roubin?' he said stiffly.

She half sat up, leaning back, her hands clutching the hot dry sand, as she stared at him in dismay. He was angry, furiously angry. Only that could explain the stiffness, the icy quietness of his manner.

She stared along the blinding white sand and almost envied the small children happily digging castles. If only Deborah was about. if only someone would interrupt them before Roland Harvey began to scold her.

He was sitting very upright by her side, his eyes fixed on her gravely. For once he was not wearing sunglasses and his blue-grey eyes looked almost green.

'Take off your sunglasses,' he snapped suddenly. Startled, she obeyed. He leaned forward, still looking at her.

'That's better. Those wretched things make

it impossible to know what a person is thinking,' he said, still curtly. 'I've come to apologize to you for my rudeness yesterday, Miss Roubin,' he went on stiffly.

She stared at him in amazement. 'But—'

He lifted his hand. 'It was very rude of me. I should have realized how very sensitive young people are about their youth. I do apologize and hope you can forgive me.' He paused. 'I realize, Miss Roubin, that you are a woman, and—that you are ready for love.' His voice was solemn, but there was a twinkle in his eyes.

She found herself blushing, but she had to smile. 'It's very generous of you, Mr. Harvey, but I'm the one who should apologize,' she said.

'Forgiven?' he asked lightly, and held out his hand.

'Well, we've both apologized, and are we both forgiven?'

She put her hand in his and felt his strong lean fingers close over hers for a moment. She shivered. Why, he was nice, so very, very nice.

'Now we'll forget it, shall we?' He smiled. 'I'm afraid I must go now, for I have an appointment, but I had to speak to you first. Explain to Deborah for me, will you? It isn't easy trying to learn a new job,' he said gravely, and she saw that he was worried. 'There's much more to running an hotel than I realized.'

'Doesn't Miss Hunter take all those things

off your shoulders? I thought that was what a manager was for,' Lauren said timidly.

'Miss Hunter is extremely efficient.' His voice was crisp. 'At times, a little . . . Well, there are certain aspects I intend to keep under my control,' he said sternly, and Lauren wondered what he had been going to say about Miss Hunter before he thought better of it. 'I feel that both my uncle and I made a grave mistake in not knowing the staff personally. There are so many of them, and Miss Hunter always engaged them . . . but maybe if I knew them better, I might discover why so many of them leave.'

Lauren studied his worried face and wondered if she should tell him that she knew the reason. He was a strange man of varying moods. He might take offence, tell her it was none of her business—might even think she had been snooping.

'Why don't you ask the members of the staff?' she suggested.

Roland Harvey turned to look at her, his face surprised.

'Now why on earth didn't I think of that? A straightforward question that only requires a simple answer. Thank you, Miss Roubin.' He smiled at her. 'I'll be seeing you,' he added, as he stood up with graceful ease and looked down on her. 'Thank you, Miss Roubin,' he said again, and walked across the sand with his usual easy stride.

She lay flat on her back, sliding on her sunglasses, pulling the big white straw hat over her eyes. He had apologized to her. She could not get over it. The famous Roland Harvey apologizing to her! It simply showed what a fine man he really was.

Somehow it made everything else much worse. The deception, which had ceased to trouble her, now seemed terrible. He had been so understanding about her dislike of being teased about her age, though, so surely he would understand the predicament Miss Cartwright had been in? It would be so much easier to tell him the truth than to wait for him to find out.

'Miss Woubin, I'm sowwy I'm so late, but I had to have my hair done,' Deborah cried eagerly.

Lauren lifted her hat and smiled. 'Hi, darling.' Deborah turned round slowly. 'Do you like my hair?' she asked anxiously.

Lauren smiled. 'I think it's lovely,' she said, but it was not true.

Deborah was short and a little too thin, her face wistful, the freckles on her nose standing out. Her sandy hair had been cut short and curled; unfortunately it was frizzy and it looked silly, almost as if the child's mother was trying to force the duckling to become a swan.

'It's most fashionable,' Lauren went on, knowing this would please Deborah most.

Deborah beamed. 'I've got a cap to keep the

90

curls dry. Can we swim? My fwiend will be here soon.'

'He left you a message,' Lauren said, and gave it.

'I saw him just now, but he didn't say,' Deborah began, her lower lip trembling. 'My mummy was cwoss with him about something, but she wouldn't *be* cwoss with him, but perhaps he felt it. She's often cwoss with him. Do you think that would make him hate me?'

Lauren hugged the small warm body to her. 'He couldn't hate you, darling, ever. Why, only the other day he told me how much he loved you.'

They were soon in the warm lagoon, playing about, splashing one another, Deborah learning now to float. Lauren was conscious of her own deep happiness. She wanted to laugh and sing and dance. He had been so nice to her . . . so very nice.

The same mood buoyed her up throughout the day and helped her through the long arduous practice in the afternoon. That night was to be a Carnival Ball and tremendous preparations for it were being made. Nick and Natalie were to dance three dances as usual, but tonight each one was to be in a different costume, so a tiny closet of a room had been allocated to Natalie to make it easier for her to make quick changes, and Claudia, the little maid, was to be in attendance.

'You're feeling all right again?' Nick asked,

91

staring down at the wide-eyed excited girl at his side.

She smiled radiantly. 'I feel wonderful.'

He looked at her as if going to ask what had changed her so much, but there wasn't time, then.

It was absurd how much Roland Harvey's gesture meant to her. Lauren kept telling herself that there was no real reason to feel so happy. But it meant a great deal to her. It meant that at last—at long last—Roland Harvey saw her as an individual, and not just a sort of shadowy person who was very young and simply Deborah's friend.

The ballroom was beautifully decorated, great garlands of exotic flowers filling the room with sweetness. Nearly all the guests were in fancy costume.

As Lauren waited with Nick for the roll of the drums that always heralded their entrance, she felt tense with a new heady excitement. Tonight she would dance as she had never danced before, she would show Roland Harvey how well she could dance, for she was sure he would be there. He would see what a good dancer she was . . .

Hastily she amended her thoughts to 'a good dancer with Nick'. It was Nick who helped her, Nick who had taught her everything, Nick who, with his trust in her, gave her such confidence.

Nick was smiling at her. 'You look smashing,

honey child,' he said.

She laughed. 'You look pretty smooth yourself, Nick.'

He did. He looked very handsome indeed. He was dressed as a fisherman, his limbs were stained dark brown, his whole make-up was elaborately 'natural'. She was a mermaid, in a tight bodice of over-lapping green scales, a skirt made to look like a tail, deceptively tight, and made of the softest green gleaming silk. She wore a green wig, and would be wearing wigs all the evening, as there could be no time for changes of colour in her hair. Nick disliked her wearing wigs, as they were hot and not ideal for the sort of dances they did, but this was an occasion when it could not be helped.

The drums rolled, and Nick picked her up effortlessly and swung her over his shoulder, striding out on to the floor with his 'capture'.

It was a delightful dance, Lauren thought, and she loved every moment of it, sliding over the floor, eluding the net, teasing the fisherman, enticing him, repulsing him . . . Evidently the hotel guests agreed with her, for the ballroom vibrated to the roar of applause.

There was just time for a short rest and a hasty change into the next costume and they took the floor again. This time they were two clowns, both wanting to be acrobats. The mime was very good, especially Nick's, Lauren thought. It was a humorous yet wistful dance, and Lauren, eyes hidden behind her make-up, thoroughly enjoyed the tumbles and falls.

Their third dance was completely different, a romantic old-fashioned waltz, and she wore a crinoline frock of palest blue satin which was garlanded with lovers' knots in blue ribbon. Her hair was piled high over a light framework and then dusted with powder. She wore beauty patches on her chin and on her shoulder. The music was so lovely that they seemed to dance effortlessly, sweeping round and round the ballroom gracefully, the gold and silver spotlights highlighting their movements. At last it was over, and they were taking their bows, Lauren curtseying again and again before she was allowed to escape.

In her dressing-room she had a light meal before changing into the fabulous gown she was to wear for the rest of the evening. Nick had come prepared for a costume ball. Lauren's gown was too utterly lovely, she thought ecstatically, as Claudia helped her into it. It looked so heavy, so stiff, so dignified, the thick folds of material falling gracefully, but in actual fact it was made of gossamer-light material, wired to give an impression of weight. Though the material looked like heavy velvet, it weighed so little. It was a deep warm crimson, elaborately embroidered with gold thread, and she wore a white wig and a black mask that gave her slanting 'cat's eyes'.

When Nick called for her, he was very elegant in satin doublet and gold-braided jacket.

They danced together once. She was still so radiantly happy, and Nick danced so beautifully that she closed her eyes, relaxed and enjoyed every moment of it. Afterwards, she and Nick separated, to dance with any other guests who sought them out. Lauren danced every dance. Now she knew how to be gay, how to parry remarks, how to make the hotel guests enjoy the dances. She had got used to pounding feet crushing her delicate shoes, how to make out that she was at fault if anyone tripped, how to guide the most clumsy dancer. In one interval between dances, her partner, a tall, bald-headed man in an Arab costume, pestered her to have champagne.

'Come on, don't be childish,' he teased. 'You can't just drink tomato juice. It isn't in keeping with your lovely face.'

'Please, I'd rather not have champagne,' she said. Then suddenly Nick was there, his arm round her shoulders.

'Please, Mr. Cootes, my wife really doesn't care for alcohol,' he said lightly, but there was suppressed anger in his voice. She looked up at him gratefully and thought how very handsome he was with his dark eyes and hair, his classical features and their promise of hidden strength.

The bald-headed man shrugged and looked annoyed, and at that moment, another man said: 'Hello, Harvey, nice to see you.'

Such joy filled Lauren that she turned round instantly and found herself staring straight into the unmasked eyes of Roland Harvey.

In dismay, she swung round again, feeling sick with fear. She heard him talking to someone and she felt the nails of her hands digging into her palms as she struggled for composure. As the first panic died down, she could reassure herself. He had not known her—there had been no flicker of recognition in his eyes as he stared at her. Had she forgotten she was wearing a mask? That she looked completely unlike little Lauren Roubin, friend of Deborah? No need to be afraid, so long as she could avoid speaking to him.

The next moment someone tapped her shoulder, and as she turned she saw that it was Roland Harvey himself.

'Might I have this dance?' he asked. His voice was stiffly polite, his face impassive. She was sure that he did not know who she was.

She went into his arms, and instantly her fear and stiffness vanished. Here was a man who danced very well, a man who loved to dance. It surprised her rather. Somehow in her thoughts she had always connected him with the great outdoors—with jungles and deserts and mountains—never with the glamour of a ballroom. He was not in costume but wearing a black dinner jacket and trousers, the only notes of colour being a scarlet cummerbund and matching carnation in his buttonhole.

She was startled when he suddenly spoke. 'Your dancing tonight was superb.'

Normally she would have been thrilled. Now she was afraid. She felt her cheeks were hot, and she kept her eyes demurely lowered, not certain how much protection the mask was. She was terrified of speaking, for surely he would know her voice? Yet answer him she must. She almost buried her face in his shoulder as she spoke:

'Thank you, it's very nice of you.'

He swung her round, deftly avoiding the many dancers on the crowded floor. She saw quickly that he was smiling.

'You're not much of a conversationalist,' he commented in the teasing voice she knew so well.

She pressed her face against his dinner jacket, trying to speak huskily. 'When I dance, I like to—'

'Enjoy it?' He finished the sentence for her. 'I stand reproved,' he went on, in the slightly pedantic way of speaking and which somehow seemed so right for him. 'It's a shame to spoil such perfect moments.'

He finished the dance without another word, and although she felt like the girl in the song: *I Could Have Danced All Night*, yet it was a relief when he finally took her back to Nick and left her with a bow. Nick was talking to a man, and a sudden impulse made Lauren put out her hand and touch Roland Harvey on the arm.

'Mr. Harvey . . .' she said appealingly. In that second she had made up her mind. There was something sordid and shameful in keeping up this pretence. She was sure he would understand.

But Roland Harvey was not listening. He was not even looking at her. He was staring across the room at a very beautiful woman. A beautiful woman indeed, wearing an elaborately simple dress of pleated black chiffon, the floating panels trimmed with diamante embroidery. There was a narrow tiara on her elaborately dressed hair, diamonds in her ears, at her neck. Her eyes were bright and she stood, tapping her foot impatiently and looking round her, as if waiting for someone.

Roland Harvey walked across the empty floor of the ballroom. He had eyes for only one person—the lovely Leila Lindstrom.

Close behind Lauren, Nick bent down to whisper in her ear.

'It looks as if Mrs. Lindstrom's plans might come to something, honey child,' he said softly. 'He couldn't get there fast enough!'

# CHAPTER SIX

Lauren was not sure what she had expected as a result of Roland Harvey's apology and apparent acceptance of her as a woman, but nothing whatever happened. If anything, she thought he treated her a little more distantly than before. Although every day he joined them on the sands, now he devoted most of his time to Deborah, including Lauren in the conversation but rarely addressing her personally. This puzzled her and worried her a little, but when she confided in Nick, he merely laughed.

'Just leave well alone, honey child,' he said cheerfully. He had been very pleased because Roland Harvey had not recognized her, even though he had danced with her that one unforgettable time.

One morning she overslept and hurried down to the beach, knowing how disappointed Deborah would be if she went there and found no 'Miss Woubin' waiting for her. It was a perfect day. The majestic palm trees waved slowly, the sea sparkled and danced in the sunshine, the white sands were crowded with children. How very very different this fantastic dream-come-true was from London's drab streets in winter-time. How very very lucky she was, she thought, as she hurried along the winding path that led through the flowering shrubs.

Lauren was thinking worriedly, also, about the lack of success in Mr. Harvey's approach to his staff. He had not mentioned it to her, but Rene Thompson had told Lauren with some amusement about it.

'He asked us to be frank with him and say if we were dissatisfied with our salaries or our working hours.' She had tossed her head and laughed. 'How naive can a man be? Did he really think we would tell him the truth and have the Hunter chuck us out in a few weeks' time?'

Shocked by Rene's unexpected reaction, Lauren had defended Roland Harvey. 'He wouldn't have told Miss Hunter,' she declared.

Rene had looked at her with pity. 'Isn't it time you grew up? You can be sure he would have told the Hunter and asked her about it, then he would have forgotten the whole incident and left it to the Hunter to put things right—and what would have happened? Those of us who complained would have been told politely that our services were no longer needed, or something we had done wrong would have been magnified in order to get rid of us. Oh, no,' Rene had laughed bitterly, 'we sat tight.'

So poor Mr. Harvey had failed to get any satisfaction. Lauren often wondered if she dared mention it to him, but with his new formality she had not found the courage.

As she settled herself under 'their' palm tree, Lauren heard Deborah's eager little voice and turned to watch her coming across the sands, tugging Roland Harvey with her.

'You're late,' Deborah said accusingly. 'We've been swimming.'

Roland Harvey's lean brown body was glistening from drops of water from the sea. His eyes were hidden behind his sunglasses, his hair plastered flat.

He sank down on the warm sand by her side. 'Good morning, Miss Roubin,' he said in that new formal voice that put a wall between them.

'I can dive, Miss Woubin, I can dive!' Deborah was saying excitedly as she danced round them.

Lauren could not look away from the big man. He was staring at her, too, but she could not see the expression in his eyes.

'Miss Woubin, I'm speaking to you,' Deborah said reproachfully.

With a jerk, Lauren pulled herself together and smiled at the little girl by her side. 'I'm sorry, darling, I did hear you. Can you really dive? That's wonderful.'

'Mr. Harvey says I'm going to be a weally good swimmer,' Deborah began, just as a shadow fell across Lauren's sun-kissed body. Startled, she looked up, and there was Mrs. Lindstrom, her eyes narrowed, her mouth a thin angry line.

'So there you are, Deborah,' she said crossly. 'You should have told me you were coming to the beach. I've been looking . . .' She turned to Roland Harvey, her voice changing. 'Was she with you, Roland? If so, that's quite all right.'

Even as Lauren was scrambling politely to her feet, Roland Harvey had stood up with one swift easy movement. He was half smiling.

'I'm sorry if you were alarmed, Leila. I thought you knew that if ever Deborah vanishes, she is either with me or with Miss Roubin.'

'Please sit down,' Mrs. Lindstrom said. 'I don't want to spoil anything.' She looked very beautiful in a white swimsuit.

Lauren was thinking unhappily that they were on Christian name terms, if that meant anything. How odd to call Mr. Harvey 'Roland'. It was a wonderful name and suited him perfectly. She sat down awkwardly and silently as Mrs. Lindstrom proceeded to chat to Mr. Harvey, deliberately, it seemed, leaving Lauren out of the conversation. Lauren lay back and closed her eyes, wondering how she could quietly withdraw from the scene, for she was sure that neither of them wanted her to stay. So she was surprised when Roland Harvey suddenly stood up and said:

'Time for another lesson, Deborah.'

Deborah was on her feet in a second, racing

102

down towards the edge of the lagoon, where the tiny waves crawled in so lazily.

There was a little silence after Roland Harvey had followed the small girl, and Lauren had kept her eyes tightly closed, hoping that Mrs. Lindstrom would believe her to be asleep, or would go away. No such luck!

'Miss Roubin, I want to talk to you.' Mrs. Lindstrom's voice shattered the stillness.

Reluctantly Lauren opened her eyes and met the steel blue gaze of the older woman. She sat up. 'Yes, Mrs. Lindstrom?' she said politely.

Mrs. Lindstrom leaned forward. 'When,' she asked sharply, 'are you starting that ballet class? I don't want Deborah to forget all that she has learned from you—and so very expensively.'

Lauren flushed and stifled indignant words. After all, Mrs. Lindstrom must know that Mrs. Cartwright charged the high fees; it had nothing to do with her.

'I presume the classes are going to start?' Mrs. Lindstrom continued. 'After all, that's what you are here for, isn't it?'

Lauren swallowed nervously. Was Mrs. Lindstrom getting suspicious? 'Yes, of course . . .' she began.

'Well, it's high time the classes started.' Mrs. Lindstrom frowned. 'I never see you in the hotel. Where do you sleep?'

'In the hotel, but—'

Mrs. Lindstrom nodded. It was a very good thing, Lauren thought distractedly, that Mrs. Lindstrom had a habit of answering her own questions. It helped when you didn't know what answer to give!

'Of course. Naturally you would not be allowed to use the hotel reception rooms.' There was a silence while Lauren dared to breathe a tiny sigh of relief, and then Mrs. Lindstrom continued: 'Mr. Harvey seems very fond of Deborah.'

A safe subject! 'Oh, he is, very fond of her,' Lauren could say fervently and truthfully. 'He's wonderful with her.'

Mrs. Lindstrom was watching the two figures gambolling happily in the lagoon. 'Deborah is fond of him, too. He will make a good father.'

She spoke so complacently, so . . . so surely, that Lauren felt as if something inside her was cringing. So it was true; Deborah was right. Roland Harvey was going to marry Leila Lindstrom.

Lauren was suddenly aware that Mrs. Lindstrom was looking at her.

'Miss Roubin,' Mrs. Lindstrom began slowly, 'you are very young, and as an older woman I feel I ought to offer you a few words of advice.' She paused.

Lauren clenched her hands, tensing herself for what was to come. Such an introduction usually meant something nasty was about to be said! 'Yes, Mrs. Lindstrom,' she said meekly.

'Mr. Harvey is a very kind man,' Mrs. Lindstrom said slowly, opening her beach bag and taking out a silver cigarette case. She took her time over lighting her cigarette, and Lauren had to keep very still, fighting the sudden urge to jump to her feet and run away. 'A very kind, patient man,' Mrs. Lindstrom continued slowly. 'It would be a pity if you misinterpreted that kindness.'

Lauren stared at her. 'I—What do you mean?' she asked.

Mrs. Lindstrom gave a thin smile. 'Simply that you are very young. Deborah happens to have taken a fancy to you and therefore you have been thrown into Mr. Harvey's company. Normally you would never have met him. Naturally he looks upon you as Deborah's young friend.' Her voice rasped suddenly. 'I wouldn't like you to be hurt because you misunderstood his behaviour.'

Lauren's mouth went dry. Somehow she swallowed, somehow she found voice enough to say: 'I'm not likely to misunderstand his behaviour, Mrs. Lindstrom. I realize that to Mr. Harvey I'm merely a child.' She could not keep the bitterness out of her voice, and was uncomfortably aware of the quick flicker of interest in Mrs. Lindstrom's eyes. 'If you'll excuse me now—' Lauren said, scrambling to her feet, gathering her belongings and escaping along the twisting path to the hotel.

In her room, she changed into a demure white cotton frock that intensified her youthful appearance. Her hands were trembling so much that it was difficult to do up the zip fastener. She brushed her hair so that it fell into a long page-boy bob, curling under at the ends. She leaned close to the mirror and surveyed her tearful eyes. It was foolish to get so worked up about it, she told herself. Maybe Mrs. Lindstrom had meant it kindly. But did it mean that Mrs. Lindstrom had guessed one of her secrets—that she loved Roland Harvey? Or far, far worse still, had Roland Harvey been embarrassed by her and mentioned it to Mrs. Lindstrom, asking her assistance?

That was a terrible, unbearable thought. But why should he? When had she ever done or said anything that could have embarrassed him?

She went down to Miss Hunter's office. Somehow she must arrange about the ballet class before Mrs. Lindstrom had time to ask Miss Hunter questions. How terrible it would be if it was Mrs. Lindstrom who told Roland Harvey the truth about Natalie Natal, the dancer.

Miss Hunter's office was small but luxurious. Great jars of scented flowers stood about, but her desk was neat and bare. She looked at Lauren impatiently.

'Now what do you want?' she snapped.

Stumbling over the words, Lauren explained

the situation.

'I'm afraid she might guess the truth,' she concluded.

'Really,' Miss Hunter said, and there was no mistaking the hostility in her eyes, 'you can hardly expect me to go on protecting you indefinitely.' Her pencil gave an impatient tattoo on the polished desk.

Lauren bit her lip nervously. Maybe she should have let Nick handle this. He seemed to be able to get on well with Miss Hunter. 'I thought if I could have a ballet class for the children on the sands . . .' she stammered.

In the end Miss Hunter consented. 'Naturally you can't expect payment for it.' Her voice was tart. 'It had better be on the family beach every morning at half-past ten. I'll notify the parents and let you have a list of pupils. Start tomorrow—and no missing a class just because you don't feel like it,' she finished sternly.

'Of course not, Miss Hunter,' Lauren said meekly. 'Thank you.'

Outside the office door, she lifted her hands to her hot cheeks. Why did Miss Hunter hate her so? What had she done to deserve it?

'Miss Roubin,' a familiar deep voice said.

Lauren jumped and stared up into the face of Roland Harvey. He had changed into a tropical suit; he looked very well-groomed, his dark red hair smooth, his blue-grey eyes frankly curious. 'What on earth are you doing here?' he went on.

How fortunate that she could tell the truth. It would be difficult to lie with those searching eyes gazing into hers.

'I was seeing Miss Hunter about the ballet class I'm going to give to the children,' she explained.

He nodded. 'Oh, I see. Yes, Mrs. Lindstrom was telling me about it. Deborah will enjoy it.'

'Oh, yes, she's very good, very good indeed.' Lauren stopped talking, suddenly aware that her very nervousness might make him suspicious. She smiled vaguely and slipped by him, escaping to her room, deciding to finish her letter sitting on the balcony.

In the morning, she had ten pupils on the sands; in less than a week, she had thirty, all little girls in sun-suits or swimsuits. There could be no question of devoting the time to ballet alone, so she taught them the basic positions and some steps, and also gave them lessons in Greek dancing—anything that was rhythmic and graceful. She often wondered what Miss Hunter charged for the lessons, but as she herself was getting nothing, it did not really interest her, and most of the parents seemed delighted to have their small girls taken off their hands for an hour each morning.

As the days passed, her life seemed to have settled down into a steady and pleasant routine. Since she began giving the dancing lessons in the morning she rarely saw Roland Harvey, for he seldom joined them in the short time she had before the afternoon's practice. Everything went smoothly, Nick being in a good mood, though a little quiet.

Then came the night they danced their French Doll dance. It was the first time she had danced it, and Lauren did not like it when they practised it. It was to be the third and final dance of the evening.

The first dance was a new kind of tango, a rapid, spirited dance; their second dance that night was a lively one-step; and as Claudia helped her to dress for the French Doll dance, Lauren felt tired and depressed. It was a very hot day, an oppressive sort of evening, with clouds banking in the sky and the lagoon looking almost oily in its stillness. There was a sultriness in the atmosphere that was heavy and made her feel exhausted. Also, she confessed to herself, it was partly because it had been such a very depressing day. It was Deborah's birthday, and Lauren had taken her presents down with her to the beach, but Deborah was not in the class that day. However, later, lying under their palm tree, she had been so sure the child would turn up that, as the hours passed and there was no sign of Deborah or of Roland Harvey, her thoughts began to imagine all sorts of things. Had Roland Harvey taken Deborah and her mother out for the day . . . perhaps on one of the many yachts that were in the harbour? She packed up the small embroidered handbag she had made for Deborah, and the gaily coloured story book, and thought the day would never end.

But it did, and here she was, dressing for the third and last dance of the evening and wishing herself a few hundred miles away!

The stiffly starched petticoats and pale blue frock with the large sash, the long white socks and the shiny black, flat-heeled shoes made a very different costume from what she usually wore when dancing. She adjusted the wig of golden curls that framed her face, a last dab of powder on her nose, a quick worried look at the reflection of the French Doll, with a white face and two blobs of scarlet in her cheeks, a cupid's bow of a mouth. All very neat and prim. She moved her arms and legs stiffly as Nick had taught her.

Nick was waiting by the open doorway to the ballroom, hidden from view by the heavy folds of the cream and gold brocade curtains. Joining him, she thought how comical he looked in his exaggerated French costume; his moustache and beard changing him completely, his white kid gloves, his black pointed shoes, his black silk suit. They stood together, waiting for the drums to roll, gazing at the crowded tables, each one lit by pink and gold candles. The usual clatter of sound—chatter, laughter, clatter of dishes, music. Suddenly the roll of drums—a sudden silence . . .

Lauren had her hand through Nick's arm and she felt his body stiffen suddenly.

'What is it, Nick?' she asked. Her nerves, already taut from tiredness, seemed to be stretched to breaking point.

He turned to her almost roughly. 'Nothing at all. Come on, or we'll miss our cue.'

But his quick movement was too late, for already she had seen the table by the floor and recognized its occupants.

The ballroom was plunged into black darkness and the spotlight focused its shaft of blinding light on them as they danced on to the floor. She moved like an automaton and was aware that Nick was almost carrying her and that her legs were far more stiff than they were supposed to be.

She danced as if dazed, trying hard to remember all Nick had taught her, knowing she was not helping him at all with the lifts.

Seated at that table had been Roland Harvey, Mrs. Lindstrom and . . . and Deborah.

It was the sight of Deborah that had filled Lauren with such fear. You might fool grown-ups—but rarely children.

As Nick lifted her and swung her round, he said in a harsh whisper, 'Pull yourself together. They won't know you.'

Her feet touched the ground and she went through the routine pantomime of walking away stiffly, her every movement expressive of her contempt for the man who had purchased her from the doll shop. She drew several long deep breaths, resolutely looking away from the direction of that certain table. No, Nick was right. Deborah would not know her. It would never enter the child's head that this could be her *Miss Woubin.* To Deborah, this would simply be a part of an exciting day spent with her adored Roland Harvey.

She missed a step and Nick had to cover up for her by improvising, and then, gratefully, she realized that the music was coming to a close. Nick's hand was warm on hers as he led her forward to bow. She gave a stiff curtsey and then bowed as the applause rippled through the crowded room. She could see the table as the lights in the ballroom blazed. Deborah was clapping excitedly, her little freckled face radiant. Roland was lighting a cigarette and handing it to Mrs. Lindstrom.

And then, suddenly, Deborah was on her feet.

As she ran across the room, and in the sudden silence, her voice came shrill and clear.

'Why, it's Miss Woubin . . . my Miss Woubin!'

# CHAPTER SEVEN

Deborah's voice sounded clear and loud in the suddenly quiet ballroom. Lauren's first impulse was to turn and run, her second to tell Deborah that she was wrong—and then, looking down into the child's upturned, excited little face, she knew that she could do none of these things.

'Why, darling,' Lauren said quietly, bending down and taking the child's hand in hers. 'Many happy returns of the day. Have you had a lovely birthday?'

'Oh, it was tewwibly good fun, Miss Woubin,' Deborah said excitedly. 'Mr. Harvey, my fwiend, took us out and—'

'Darling, tell me about it tomorrow,' Lauren said gently. 'Your mummy is waiting for you.'

Deborah seemed to realize for the first time that she was the centre of attraction and that everyone was watching her. For a moment her mouth quivered and she looked very small and very scared.

Lauren squeezed her hand. 'We'll curtsey to the people, Deborah, just like we do on the stage, and then I'll take you back to your mummy.'

Deborah beamed. 'You'll curtsey, too?'

'Of course.' Lauren managed to laugh. 'So will Nick. Deborah, may I introduce my partner, Nick, to you?' she went on with special formality, for she knew it would make Deborah feel important. Lauren had seen the surprise, dismay and anger on Nick's face, but she knew that whatever happened, this little incident must be treated normally or else the child would be badly frightened.

Nick accepted the situation, bowing before Deborah, lifting her hand very formally to his mouth. 'At your service, mademoiselle,' he said, with an atrocious French accent. Then he smiled. 'You recognized Miss Roubin at once?'

There was a stillness about his voice that frightened Lauren although he was still smiling.

'Oh, no, I didn't,' Deborah said eagerly. 'She looked so diffewent, sort of funny.' She turned immediately to Lauren and her face was apologetic. 'Nicely funny, Miss Woubin.'

'But then how did you know her?' Nick persisted.

Deborah laughed happily. This was probably, to her, just an exciting ending to the most wonderful birthday she had ever had. '

' 'Cos she stood just like a stork. She always does when she's tired,' Deborah said triumphantly.

Lauren stared down at her with dismay in her face and she heard Nick catch his breath.

'Come on, Deborah darling,' she said hastily. 'Come and curtsey and then we must take you back to Mummy.'

The three of them took a step forward and while Nick bowed, Deborah and Lauren curtseyed. Deborah looked instantly at Lauren.

'Did I do that all wight? I didn't fall over.'

'You did it beautifully, darling,' Lauren told her. Somehow she forced her legs to move and made herself walk across the ballroom to the table where Leila Lindstrom was sitting, bolt upright, her face cold and angry, and Roland Harvey was on his feet, as if hesitating whether or not to go to Deborah's rescue. As soon as she judged she was near enough to them to feel able to leave Deborah on her own, but far enough away to avoid a scene, Lauren bent down, lifted Deborah's hand and rested her cheek on it for a moment.

'Run along, poppet,' she said gently. 'I'll see you tomorrow.'

As Deborah trotted dutifully forward, Lauren turned back to join Nick and there was a further round of applause before they could leave the ballroom.

Once safely out of sight, Nick gripped her shoulders and shook her. 'You little idiot! Now see what a spot your stupid trick has landed us in!'

Lauren battled with tears. She was still shivering with the shock and the need to behave normally. 'I'm so terribly sorry,' she whispered.

'It's too late to say you're sorry,' he scolded

her. 'You and your stupid infatuation for that man . . . making such a fuss of the kid . . . I ought to have known this would happen!'

'Please, Nick,' she caught hold of his arm, 'I've said I'm sorry.' He looked down into the tear-filled eyes, looked at the trembling mouth. 'Please, Nick, can I go to bed? I don't feel I can face—'

His face was hard. 'No, I'm afraid you can't. We've got to face the music together. Why should I shoulder all the blame when it's your own pig-headed stupidity that's landed us in such a mess?' He paused. 'Go and get changed,' he said curtly. 'I'll wait for you.'

She changed quickly into an elegant silken Grecian gown that normally she loved, but tonight she could only think of the moment when she must face Roland Harvey's steely, accusing eyes.

Nick was waiting for her, immaculate in tails; he apologized stiffly. 'Maybe I shouldn't have let fly at you like that, Lauren. You were as upset as I was, but everything seemed to be going so smoothly, and then . . .' He smiled wryly. 'Maybe you should see a psychiatrist about this stork image of yours. Was your knee aching?'

'I don't know. I think I was frightened because I'd seen Deborah with them—and I never did like that French Doll dance and—and I was a bit tired. Oh, Nick, I never know I'm doing it,' she finished desperately.

116

His smile was twisted. 'So you unconsciously comforted yourself and gave the game away. Well, it's done, so no good holding a court martial. You didn't mean to do it, I know. Anyhow,' he said more cheerfully, 'we may be exaggerating it all. Perhaps your friendship with the child may have some influence on Roland Harvey's reaction. Come on, we'd better go in and dance.'

She was stiff in his arms as they circled the crowded floor and she searched nervously for Roland Harvey. After ten minutes, she was sure he was not there and she could breathe more easily. Nor did she see any sign of Mrs. Lindstrom or Deborah.

'They're probably putting the child to bed,' Nick said, as he fetched her a tomato juice. 'I'm sorry for the kid, with a mother like that.'

'You don't like Mrs. Lindstrom?' Lauren asked, as she sipped the drink. There were still butterflies tumbling around inside her. The bad moment had only been postponed, she knew that; the moment when Roland Harvey would look at her, knowing she was a liar.

Nick laughed. 'You can say that again! It's no lie. She's a real menace, that woman. She's had a dozen dancing lessons from me already and has something of a crush on me.' His eyes crinkled with laughter as he smiled at Lauren. 'You've no idea how much charm I can turn on!'

Lauren looked at him. 'I don't know how

you can bear to do it,' she said honestly.

He shrugged. 'One has to earn a living, and it isn't always easy.' His face clouded. 'I had a letter from Natalie today. She's rather depressed, poor girl. The doctor says she's fine physically but her mental outlook is all wrong. She's convinced she'll never dance again, that I shall fall in love with some glamorous dame . . . Her letter was just dreary with moans.'

'She's missing you.'

'I suppose so, but it isn't anyone's fault. Anyway, honey child, what I'm getting at is that the fact is I'm out to earn every penny I can to give Natalie a holiday which will put her back on her feet. She just needs some sunshine, some fun and excitement, and me.' He screwed up his face humorously. 'Me—the great lover! But it isn't easy to save, what with Miss Hunter taking a percentage of every penny I earn.'

'But, Nick,' Lauren said quickly, 'that isn't fair.'

'Very little in life is fair,' Nick said, more cheerfully. 'Let's dance once more and then we'll split up, honey child. I don't think we need worry about tonight, for I expect Mr. Harvey will send for us in the morning.'

The rest of the evening sped by quite pleasantly. Lauren came in for a lot of teasing, especially from the fathers she had been introduced to as Deborah's friend, 'Miss Woubin'. But no one seemed annoyed about

118

the deception. Several thought it a good idea. As one man said to her: 'A dancer has to be glamorous, artificial and a little mysterious. I can quite see it must be a bit of an effort to keep that up all day long.'

'I am really Lauren Roubin,' she told him. 'And I work for the Cartwright School of Dancing, and I was only sent here because the real Natalie Natal was ill.'

She only hoped, without much hope, that Roland Harvey would take the same view as these men.

In the morning she awaited the expected summons. She stayed in her room, for Nick had said that when they were sent for it would be good policy not to keep the great man waiting! She waited and waited, sitting on the balcony, gazing at the lovely view, wondering how much longer she would be there to see it, thinking about cold drab London and the shame of being sent home like a naughty schoolgirl . . . But worst of all was the thought of never seeing Roland Harvey again, never having the chance to speak to him, to look at him.

She had her lunch sent up to her room, afraid lest she miss the dreaded summons. But it did not come, and when she met Nick in the deserted ballroom for their practice, he was very depressed.

'Mr. Harvey has flown to London,' he told Lauren. 'Seems he sent for the Hunter this morning and wanted to know the truth—were you Lauren Roubin or Natalie Natal, and if you weren't, why were you here and all that sort of thing. Miss Hunter says she had no choice. She's pretty mad with us and says we've—well, made him lose trust in her. Anyhow she said it was Miss Cartwright's fault, that we arrived here and put her in an awkward position, that it would have been impossible to replace us at such short notice, also that we told her a hard-luck story about Natalie's op and, well, all in all, properly spilled the beans.'

'Was he very angry?' Lauren asked fearfully, looking round the deserted ballroom. How different it looked from what it did at night when the tables glittered with silver and glass and the sheen of starched damask and there was the clatter of plates and cutlery, and chatter and laughter.

'She says he was very quiet and startled her by announcing that he was flying to London today. He didn't say why, but it's my bet that he prefers to work at top level and will make Miss Cartwright recall us.'

'Oh, no!' Lauren said in dismay.

Nick shrugged. 'Could be. Probably he'd see it as the simplest, most pleasant way of disposing of us. He'll want to avoid any unpleasant publicity for the hotel, and if she replaces us . . .'

'How can she replace us, Nick? Who is

there?'

Nick smiled ruefully. 'Look, honey child, we could easily be replaced. Miss Cartwright is a temperamental old witch, and rather than lose Roland Harvey's goodwill and possible future engagements, she would get someone, no matter what it cost. It was only because she wanted to send out two of her regular staff that she had to choose you. We work on all-the-year-round salary, apart from a bonus for a special job like this, so it's cheaper that way. Oh, she counts the pennies all right. When I think what we must be earning for her during this three months' booking, I feel I'd like to become a freelance and chance a few months' unemployment each year.'

After the work-out, they strolled back to Lauren's room, both uneasy. 'Oh, Nick,' Lauren burst out, 'I do so hope they don't send us back.'

'So do I,' Nick admitted. 'But don't count on it. I'm expecting a cable from Miss Cartwright at any moment. Boy, will she be mad!'

In her room, Lauren hurriedly finished her letter home. She had written to tell her parents the whole story; of the deception, the discovery, and how worried she was.

*'I wanted to tell Mr. Harvey the truth, but Nick wouldn't let me,' she wrote. 'Miss Hunter seemed to think he would be very angry about it, and now he is. He*

*has rushed off to London and Nick
thinks he will make Miss Cartwright send
for us. It's all too disappointing for words,
and I shall absolutely hate leaving this
heavenly place.'*

She addressed the envelope and sealed it,
comfortingly aware that her parents would
sympathize and understand, only wishing they
were there. She saw that she had a few minutes
to spare before her appointment with the
hairdresser, and remembered her promise to
Deborah to hear all about the wonderful
birthday treat. If she was quick, she might
catch Deborah in the children's dining-room,
having her supper.

As usual there were a lot of people walking
through the lofty luxurious reception hall as
she dropped her letter in the mail box, many of
them guests newly arrived by plane or by ship,
others collecting their mail, or strolling on
their way to the Bamboo Room for cocktails or
to meet their friends. It was always a hub of
noise and laughter, and today was no
exception. As she turned from the letter box,
Lauren saw Mrs. Lindstrom staring at her.

'Please, Mrs. Lindstrom,' Lauren said, 'I
haven't been able to see Deborah today, but
would you tell her—'

Mrs. Lindstrom's face was icily cold with
distaste. 'Please, Miss Roubin—or should I say
Mrs. Natal?' she asked, her voice clear and

loud, 'I would prefer you in future to stay away from my daughter. I don't feel inclined to trust her with someone who tells lies.'

It seemed to Lauren as if there was a sudden lull in the noise around them and that everyone was looking at her. She felt her cheeks grow hot. 'Mrs. Lindstrom, I am Miss Roubin, as you know. There's an explanation for—'

'Naturally,' Mrs. Lindstrom said nastily. 'You've had time to think one up. Of course, one cannot but wonder if it's true or not . . .' She paused significantly.

'Of course it's true!'

'I see no "of course" about it. You've been lying to me all the time. You told me you had come here to teach ballet to the children and—'

'Please, Mrs. Lindstrom,' Lauren said firmly, aware that a small crowd had collected round them, their faces bright with curiosity. 'Natalie Natal had to have a severe operation and was not allowed to dance. Miss Cartwright, for whom I work, asked me to take her place. It seemed simpler to take Natalie's professional name . . .'

'And her husband?' Mrs. Lindstrom asked. Lauren's face burned. 'I happen to be Natalie's friend, and Nick—'

'Is certainly not to be trusted,' Mrs. Lindstrom said curtly. 'I happen to know that Mr. Harvey is very shocked and angry.'

'Please, Mrs. Lindstrom,' Lauren said. People were pushing closer to hear more clearly. If only the floor would open and swallow her up!

'Doubtless Mr. Harvey will deal with you,' Mrs. Lindstrom finished, and walked away.

Lauren fled to the hairdresser, and as she sat, hot and miserable, under the dryer, she thought of the ugly little scene. How Mrs. Lindstrom hated her. But why? Why should two elegant, sophisticated and beautiful women like Mrs. Lindstrom and Miss Hunter hate her? If only she knew what she had done to offend them.

If Mrs. Lindstrom was going around saying all those awful things about Nick! As for saying he was not to be trusted . . .

Small, unwelcome thoughts crowded into her mind. She remembered the men who laughed at her because she would not drink anything and who teased her about Nick's quick protection of her, and asked her if she was not jealous of her husband's affairs. She had laughed at the time and thought no more of it, for she trusted Nick implicitly. His very behaviour towards her made her trust him. But now she found herself beginning to wonder, and that frightened her. If these wispy accusations built up into something in her mind, how much more they might affect people who did not know the real Nick? He had always said that Mrs. Lindstrom was a dangerous woman. Why, she could ruin his whole future!

What could she do about it? Lauren wondered, as the little bearded hairdresser combed her hair into strange arrangements. For once he did not chatter to her. Had he also heard about it all?

That night she and Nick danced without any heart. It seemed to them both that their applause was less than usual. Afterwards when they mixed with the hotel guests, everything seemed normal and yet neither Lauren nor Nick could hide their depression.

Suppose Roland Harvey forgave them and let them stay—would it be as simple as that? Suppose he heard of the gossip going round, wouldn't he be angry with Mrs. Lindstrom for starting it? But would he know who had started it? Wasn't it more than likely that Mrs. Lindstrom herself would tell him what she had 'heard' and say how shocked she was about it?

Next day she talked to Rene Thompson.

'If only I could see Deborah . . .' she sighed.

Rene Thompson lifted one eyebrow, letting her hair swing forward as she bent to straighten a pile of towels. 'Look, stop fussing so. This is a lot of nonsense about nothing. You and Nick haven't done anything criminal, so stop getting such a complex about it,' she scolded. 'It's only a couple of women, the Hunter and Mrs. Lindstrom, who are trying to build it up into something, simply because

125

both of them are after your blood.'

'But why are they?' Lauren asked miserably.

Rene chuckled. 'Because the great Roland Harvey obviously likes you quite a bit.'

'But he doesn't like me. He sees me as a child, as a friend of Deborah's.'

'How do you know? Has he ever told you so?' Rene asked.

'Of course not, but it's the way he treats me.'

'Well, I wouldn't mind being treated like that by the one and only Roland Harvey,' Rene said, and laughed. 'There's always the chance that one day he may wake up and see what you are really like, and then—wham!—just like that, he'll fall at your feet, a helpless slave to your beauty!'

'Oh, Rene, stop teasing me,' Lauren said, laughing helplessly. Rene had a knack of cheering her up. Then she remembered Deborah. 'But how is the child?'

Rene looked sober for a moment and a little sad. 'Poor kid, my heart bleeds for her, Lauren. With a mother like that . . . It seems she has been crying so much that they had to have the doctor in, for the child got quite hysterical. I don't know what over . . . unless her mother says she must never speak to you again.'

'If only there was something I could do,' Lauren said.

*     *     *

It was to be three days before they knew anything definite, three days of slow mental torture, of tense nerves and quick tempers; three days of not seeing Deborah, of worrying about her and being unable to do anything about it; three days during which Nick grew daily more depressed; three days of Miss Hunter's angry glares; of feeling heavy and clumsy and miserable.

Then someone told them that Roland Harvey had returned from England.

'He'll send for us in the morning, I expect,' Nick said that evening before they danced. Both felt as if they were dancing on red-hot wires, and nothing went right, and although they tried to avoid the subject of what was going to happen to them, every time they talked together the conversation seemed to return to the same thing. If only they knew!

The whole evening both were conscious that it might be their last night there—the last time they danced to this warm, responsive audience.

That night Lauren stood on her balcony, looking at the stars sparkling in the dark sky, at the distant water, the silhouette of palm trees. This lovely place . . .

In the morning she got up early and went straight to Deborah's palm tree. Nick had told her not to hang about the hotel.

'We don't want to look like whipped dogs,'

he had said, 'even if we feel like it,' he had added with a grin. 'Strictly speaking, you and I are not at fault. The blame really rests on Miss Cartwright. I've some dancing lessons to give in the morning, so I'll be around, and I'll know where you are in case I have to send for you.'

So Lauren lay on her towel on the warm sand, listening to the strange rustles and whispers from the palm tree above her. Everything that day seemed to look more beautiful than it had ever looked before. The colours were brighter—the sea looked more blue—the cloudless sky was perfect. Laughter and voices drifted towards her—everyone seemed to be so happy. It was the loveliest place for a holiday. At least she had seen it and enjoyed it for a while.

She had hoped that perhaps Mrs. Lindstrom might now have relented, or Deborah persuaded Roland Harvey to help her, but although Lauren waited under the palm tree until it was time to give her dancing lesson to the children, and then hurried back to it afterwards, there was no sign of Deborah.

Had they really done such a terrible thing? she asked herself. Wasn't it being exaggerated out of all normal proportions?

Rene Thompson thought so, but she had pointed out that not telling the truth to Mr. Harvey had at least given them a chance to enjoy a few weeks' sunshine there.

If only that was all it had been . . . just a very

pleasant way to work. If only Roland Harvey had not walked into her life . . .

She turned over, loving the warmth of the sun on her back, and suddenly she saw Nick come striding across the sands towards her.

She sat up hastily. Nick was too far away for her to see his expression. He waved. She waved back, not sure if he was beckoning to her or merely waving. She held her breath and crossed her fingers tightly. Oh, please, let it be good news!

Nick began to run towards her. How handsome he looked, tall and lean, neat in his tropical suit, his dark hair gleaming. As he got closer, she saw the excitement on his face.

'It's all right,' he called out. 'We can stay.'

She closed her eyes for a second as relief swept through her. It was all right. All right!

Nick flung himself down beside her and seized her hands.

'It's all right, honey child,' he said excitedly, smiling at her. 'Mr. Harvey says we can stay. He saw Miss Cartwright and everything is okay.' Nick's eyes were bright with triumph. 'Of course the old Hunter is trying to make out that she talked him into forgiving us, but I don't believe it. Roland Harvey isn't the type of man to be persuaded by any woman.'

Lauren's eyes were like stars. 'Oh, how wonderful, Nick! I knew he would understand.'

Nick laughed. 'You always said so, kiddo. I wish I'd taken your advice in the first place.

The last few days have been like a nightmare.'

Lauren sighed. 'They most certainly have! Now we can relax. You saw Mr. Harvey?'

'Oh, no, of course not. As the Hunter pointed out politely, we're small fry to a great man like that. He instructed Miss Hunter to inform me that while he regretted my wife's inability to fulfil her share of the contract, he was more than satisfied with the substitute provided.' He squeezed her hands tightly. 'You've been a good kid, Lauren—worked hard and never moaned, done really well! Just wait until I tell Miss Cartwright. After this, you need never go back to teaching kids how to dance.'

Suddenly he leaned forward, put both his hands on her shoulders and kissed her gently. 'That's for all you've done to help me,' he said. 'Bless you, honey child . . .'

Lauren heard a sound, and she looked over Nick's shoulder and saw Roland Harvey, standing there. He might have been there for just one moment or for longer, but without doubt he had seen Nick kiss her. His mouth was a thin line, his eyes hard and angry. Before she could speak, he had turned and walked away again, his feet making no sound on the hot sand.

Lauren decided quickly to mention it to Nick. After all, the kiss had meant nothing to either of them. What a pity, though, he had chosen that moment to show his gratitude—

just when Roland Harvey was there to see it.

Nick soon left her, for he had another dancing lesson to give. He strode off, whistling cheerfully, every now and then doing a little dance as he crossed the sands.

Lauren lay back and closed her eyes. If only Nick had not kissed her . . .

Suddenly she felt she did not want to stay on the beach any longer, some of the warmth seemed to have gone out of the sun. She gathered her things together and found her way back to the hotel.

She was having an early lunch on one of the balconies when she was paged:

'Miss Roubin . . . Miss Lauren Roubin!' The small African page, immaculate in his starched white uniform, gave her a note.

She did not recognize the handwriting— thick, heavy, determined strokes, very masculine in appearance. She read the signature first and her heart seemed to leap.

*Roland Harvey.*

Then she read the note.

*'I would like to see you in my office immediately.'*

No 'please', no politeness. Just a curt order. How angry he must be!

Hastily she pushed away her now unwanted lunch and hurried to a cloakroom, looking anxiously at her peaky face, trying to rub some colour in her cheeks. No time to go upstairs for the artificial courage which a freshly made-

131

up face might have given her. She must not keep him waiting. She ran a comb hastily through her hair.

Why did he want to see her?

It could only be because he saw Nick kissing her.

Why, oh, why had Nick chosen that moment?

Nervously she knocked on Roland Harvey's office door. He called out sharply and she entered, receiving a vague impression of a very well furnished room, with a massive walnut desk, of enormous picture windows, of shelves of books . . . but her eyes were focused on one thing only—the tall, lean man standing with his back to the wonderful view, looking at her with steely blue-grey eyes. He still wore the light tropical suit he had worn on the beach, his dark red hair was smooth, his hands clasped behind his back.

'Sit down,' he barked.

Her legs suddenly felt weak and she was glad to obey. He came towards her, towering above her. His voice was cold.

'I have just been to London, and while I was there I saw Miss Cartwright.' He spoke crisply, as if rapping out orders. 'She satisfied me that you and Nicholas Natal could remain here. As you are aware, I usually insist on a married couple performing here, but on this occasion I was, after hearing the truth of the matter, prepared to waive my usual insistence. I was

132

satisfied that Miss Cartwright had been in a difficult position, that she valued the booking and did not want to embarrass us by leaving us without dancers. What I cannot understand is . . .' he paused, frowning down at her, 'why you didn't tell me the truth. We're not strangers.' He paused again. 'Are we?' he barked.

She jumped in her seat. 'Well, no, Mr. Harvey, not—'

'Of course we're not strangers,' he said impatiently. 'I thought I had grown to know you quite well. I see how mistaken I was. You appeared to be a nice girl, so kind to that unfortunate child. Sincere, honest . . . How wrong I was!'

Her cheeks hot, Lauren jumped to her feet. 'Please, Mr. Harvey, you must believe me. I wanted to tell you the truth. I knew you would understand.'

He was still staring at her, frowning a little. 'Then why didn't you tell me?'

Unconsciously she held out her hands in an appealing little gesture. 'Nick . . . Miss Hunter . . . they both said you would be very angry and—and would send us back to England.'

His face did not lose its sternness. 'Miss Hunter tells me a very different story. She says that she advised you both to make a clean breast of it and you both begged her not to tell me.'

'That's not true,' Lauren said indignantly.

She paused, swallowed, and began again. 'I know Nick was afraid of . . .'

'You weren't?'

She looked up at him. 'Of course not. I knew you would understand.'

He turned away abruptly and went to stand by the window, speaking over his shoulder without looking at her. She stood still, twisting her hands together unhappily as she watched the firm, uncompromising back.

'I saw your parents when I was in England,' he said.

She stared at his back. 'My parents?' she echoed.

'Yes. I was not satisfied about you being out here alone with this . . . this Nicholas Natal.' Roland Harvey's voice was hard. 'However, they assured me that there was no need for me to feel alarm on your behalf. They said you had been friends with the two dancers for a long time. They made me feel happier about you.'

It was as if she had been running for a very long time and could not find her voice.

'You had no right to go and see my parents.' The angry indignant words suddenly tumbled out of her mouth. 'I'm not a child. You have no right to treat me as one.'

He swung round to stare at her.

'I have every right. While you are here, I feel responsible for you. Although your parents assured me that you could look after yourself, I doubted it. I doubt it still more now,' he said harshly, his eyes bright with anger. 'In fact, I bitterly regret agreeing that you could stay on.'

Her hand flew to her mouth. Above it, her eyes were wide with distress. 'You regret it?'

'I most certainly do. Because now I remember that you told me that you were a woman, and ready for love.' The words, as he flung them angrily at her, sounded ugly. He came closer and she stared up at him, unable to move away. 'Have you forgotten, Miss Roubin,' he said and now his voice was calm, the calm of a man battling to discipline his anger, 'have you forgotten that Nicholas Natal is a married man?'

## CHAPTER EIGHT

There was a moment during which the whole world seemed to stand still for Lauren, as she stared up into the eyes of the tall, powerful, angry man. She understood now. It was that innocent kiss of Nick's that had spoiled everything.

'Of course I haven't forgotten that Nick is married,' she said, clenching her hands, trying to keep her voice steady. 'His wife is a friend of mine.'

The rugged stern face above her did not

relax. 'What difference does that make?' he demanded.

Her face burned. 'You don't fall in love with your friend's husband,' she told him angrily.

'Don't you?' Roland Harvey asked, his voice amused.

She saw that the anger had left him now. In a way, she was sorry. At least he had been angry with her, as a person. Now he had put her back in her old place, as a very young girl. 'How do you stop yourself?' he asked lightly.

She stared at him, swallowed, tried to find the right words. Suddenly there were none. Nor could she think of an answer to that simple question. If Roland Harvey had been married to her friend, would that have stopped her from falling in love with him? It all seemed so straightforward and easy until it happened to you.

She ran her tongue nervously over her dry lips. 'I . . . I . . .' she faltered.

He looked down at the heart-shaped, flushed face, at the puzzled, frightened eyes. 'Well, go on and tell me,' he said encouragingly. 'What would you do if you found yourself in love with a married man? I'm interested.'

She was twisting her hands together. 'I'd . . . I'd go away. Right away.' She stared up into his amused eyes unflinchingly.

He lifted his eyebrows. 'I see. And if, as in this case, you could not run away?'

She suddenly realized she was doing what Nick and Deborah called her 'stork trick'. Hastily she lowered her foot and saw by the amusement on Roland Harvey's face that he had also noticed. Why had he the power to make her feel so stupid and childish?

'My dear child,' he said slowly in the voice she hated most, the voice of an indulgent parent, 'I doubt very much if you know what love means.'

She took a long deep breath. In that moment, she hated him with all her heart and, at the same time, loved him to despair. She stared up into his amused eyes, and her hand ached to smooth his dark red hair . . . she longed to fling her arms round his neck and confess the truth.

Love!

Was this what every girl dreamed about? What the poets wrote about? What gained fortunes for song-writers? Was this sick, stabbing, hopeless pain, this aching to be loved . . . was this love?

She blinked her eyes, looking away from him.

'I do know what love is.' She knew that she sounded like an emotional teenager battling with her first problem, sulky, difficult.

'You're in love with someone?'

His voice was so gentle that, for a moment, she was deceived, but when she looked up at him, she saw that he was laughing at her.

She lifted her chin. 'Yes, I am in love with someone,' she said, the words starting off defiantly but somehow growing sad. It was true. She loved him. But what was the good?

His face seemed to alter in a second, almost as if a shutter had closed down over it. He turned away and spoke over his shoulder:

'I would like you to be happy, but not at someone else's expense.'

Her face felt as if it was on fire. He thought she meant that she was in love with Nick.

'Mr. Harvey, I'm not—' she began worriedly, moving towards him. Whatever happened, he must not believe that!

He looked at her, his face cold with displeasure.

'I don't think we need discuss the matter, Miss Roubin.' He frowned. 'And now if you will excuse me . . .'

He moved with his usual swift grace to the door and opened it for her.

'You won't give me a chance to explain?' she asked him.

He frowned. 'I don't think there is anything to explain.'

There was nothing else she could do but leave the room. Once the door was closed behind her, she lifted her hands to her hot face. She felt utterly exhausted.

'Please let me pass, Miss Roubin,' a crisp voice said.

Lauren lowered her hands and stared at

Miss Hunter.

'I'm sorry,' she murmured, and moved aside, uncomfortably aware that Miss Hunter had noticed the flushed cheeks, tear-filled eyes and drooping mouth before she opened the door of Mr. Harvey's office and went inside.

Hurrying to the sanctuary of her room, Lauren thought how often it happened that Miss Hunter was on the scene when anything went wrong. If she missed a step in the dance practice, you could be sure Miss Hunter would be passing through the ballroom. If she had a difficult partner to cope with during the evening's mixing with the guests, there would be Miss Hunter, with her cold critical eyes. It was as if Miss Hunter was always watching her—which was absurd.

She had just bathed her face in cold water and was trying to hide the traces of tears when the bedroom door suddenly opened and Miss Hunter walked into the room.

Dismayed, Lauren looked in the mirror and saw Miss Hunter's reflection. She turned round, still holding the lipstick in her hand.

Miss Hunter looked regally beautiful in a deceptively simple lime green shantung suit, a diamond cluster brooch on one lapel. Her eyes were unfriendly.

'I think, Miss Roubin, that you owe me an apology,' she said.

'I do . . .' Lauren felt flustered. 'I'm sorry if I have . . .'

Miss Hunter came closer. 'You have put me in a very awkward position with Mr. Harvey. He considers that it was my duty to tell him the truth. I supposed you preferred to wait until you had wormed yourself into his confidence.' Her voice was ugly as she went on. 'Sly—that's the only word to describe you. So sweet and innocent-looking, underneath so sly and cunning. Sucking up to Roland Harvey, using that impossible child as a weapon. I wouldn't be surprised to learn that it was all a put-up job and that you arranged with Natalie Natal for her to be ill so that you could come here in her place and get your hands on the wealthy and famous Roland Harvey.' Her voice had been steadily rising as she spoke.

Lauren took a step back with the shock of the unexpected attack. 'That's not true,' she whispered.

'Truth—what do you know or care about truth?' Miss Hunter almost screamed. 'Lies, lies all the time. But I tell you one thing, my girl, it won't get you anywhere. Roland Harvey is no fool. He can see through predatory little guttersnipes like you.' For a moment her face was twisted into a hideous mask of hatred. Her whole appearance of dignity had vanished. And as Lauren stared at her, aghast, she saw Miss Hunter swallow convulsively and rush from the room, slamming the door behind her.

Lauren almost stumbled to a chair and collapsed into it. She felt unclean, as if

140

someone had thrown a bucket of slimy, evil-smelling mud over her.

She buried her face in her hands, remembering the terrible things Miss Hunter had said to her.

Worming her way into his confidence . . .

Sucking up to him . . .

Using that impossible child as a weapon . . .

Did Miss Hunter really believe those terrible accusations? It was the last straw. Lauren longed to fling all her clothes into a suitcase and catch the first plane back to dear safe England. She longed for her family and their love. Why did Miss Hunter hate her so much?

She suddenly saw the time. She was already late for practice. Nick would be furious. Hastily she grabbed her shoes and almost ran from the room.

Nick was not furious but impatient. He was arguing with the band about the correct tempo of the dance he had planned.

It was pure ballet and Lauren knew the dance well, but that afternoon her feet seemed to be all thumbs.

'But, Lauren,' Nick said patiently for the hundredth time, 'you know very well that as I put my hands round your waist, you change your weight on to the other foot. You know that as I lift you . . .'

'I do know,' Lauren said unhappily. 'I just can't seem to dance this afternoon.'

He looked at her flushed, distressed face and said they would try it through once more. 'Don't worry, honey child,' he said kindly. 'You'll be all right tonight.'

The next time it went perfectly, and Nick beamed approval.

'My knee seems to be funny,' Lauren said.

Nick laughed outright. 'Look, honey child, that knee hasn't troubled you for years, so why should it worry you today of all days?'

There seemed to be no answer to that, so Lauren merely smiled.

They had time for a welcome cold drink before Lauren went to the hairdresser.

'What's biting you, Lauren?' Nick asked, his eyes narrowed as he looked at her unhappy face.

She told him. Everything.

Her cheeks suddenly hot, she said: 'I know that was just a brotherly kiss, Nick, and it meant nothing, but . . .'

His lean humorous face was grave. 'Was it?' he asked quietly.

She stared at him in dismay. 'But of course it was, Nick. You love Natalie . . .'

He gave a twisted smile and stubbed out his cigarette with a quick impatient movement. 'Of course I do. I love her dearly, as you say. I take it that Mr. Harvey thinks you're in love with me?'

Lauren nodded. 'But that isn't all,' she said.

She told him about the ugly scene with Miss

Hunter.

'It was as if she had—gone mad, or something. The way she looked at me, Nick. Why does she hate me so?'

He leaned across the table and took her hands in his. His voice was grave. 'Look, Lauren, please don't let an old faggot like the Hunter get you down. She only hates you because she's jealous—jealous because she thinks I'm in love with you.' He smiled reassuringly into her horrified eyes. 'But you know that I'm not, don't you, honey child? You know I love Natalie. Right? Right! Miss Hunter behaved like that because that's the real Hunter, with the blinds up. The sophisticated dignified woman we see around the hotel isn't the real woman—that's just a carefully controlled pose, but let her lose her temper and she acts like a fishwife. I've seen her.' He frowned. 'Look, try to forget it, kid. We know she can't help being like that. She's just frustrated, that's all.'

'But why should she be frustrated and jealous of me when she's so beautiful?' Lauren asked.

'You think she's beautiful?' Nick said thoughtfully. 'I don't. She might be if there was more warmth in her face, more heart in her smile. She's like an icicle, with jagged dangerous spikes.' His face softened as he looked at the girl facing him, with her troubled, bewildered eyes. 'She's not one tenth

143

as beautiful as you are, Lauren.'

'Me?' Lauren cried, startled. 'Beautiful?'

Nick nodded. 'You most certainly are. Since we came out here, you seem to have matured, blossomed.' He smiled. 'It isn't due to my charm, unfortunately.'

'But, Nick, you must be teasing me. I've never been beautiful,' Lauren said wonderingly. She had never wanted to be beautiful—but quite suddenly she longed to be beautiful . . . in Roland Harvey's eyes.

'I think you are,' Nick said, rising, touching her lightly on the shoulder. 'And so do a great many other people. Now you'd better get going or we shall have Henri on our trail.'

Sitting patiently in the hairdressing salon while Henri gave her hair a black rinse, Lauren thought of Nick's words. They seemed to wrap round her heart warmly, easing a little of the hurt caused by Miss Hunter's violent attack.

Was it true? Was she really beautiful, she wondered, as she gazed at the reflection of herself in the mirror, while the hairdresser stood back, rubbing his hands, looking pleased with himself.

Lauren stared at a stranger—a woman with jet black hair that was brushed back smoothly and knotted low on her neck. A woman with large thoughtful eyes and a tender mouth.

Was that how Roland Harvey saw her?

She hurried back to her room and the

waiting bath, telling herself to stop dreaming, it was very doubtful if Roland Harvey saw her at all!

As the drums rolled that night and Nick led her out on to the ballroom floor, Lauren's heart raced as she saw Roland Harvey sitting alone, at a table near the dance floor.

She wanted Roland Harvey to find her beautiful . . . she wanted him to see her as a wonderful dancer . . . she wanted his love.

Dreams—foolish hopeless dreams.

She pirouetted on her points with her arms out-stretched, and Nick's hands lightly held her waist as the dance began. The white tutu spread out round her hips; her long slim legs were in white tights. She was all white, her black hair the only different note. Nick wore black tights and a shirt.

Everything went smoothly until she saw Roland Harvey stand up. Spinning round and round, feeling the light touch of Nick's hand on hers, she stopped in an arabesque and saw that Roland Harvey was talking to Mrs. Lindstrom. Nick's hands were at her waist as she spun round to face him and the last part of the dance, the tricky part, began . . .

It all happened so swiftly. She was reminding herself to change her weight, as Nick swept her high in the air above his head, and then she felt her toes touch the ground and . . .

She fell headlong to the ground. For a

moment she must have blacked out, for she heard and knew nothing until she felt herself lifted in strong arms and carried out of the ballroom. Opening her eyes, she found her face very near Roland Harvey's. His face was stern, his mouth a thin line as he carried her and laid her on a couch. Lauren could see Nick close behind, his face worried.

Lauren closed her eyes for a second. She heard Roland Harvey speaking, his voice vibrating with anger. 'You had no right to expect her to do that . . . she's not experienced enough. She could have been badly hurt.'

The hotel doctor was close at hand. Later she was to learn that he had hurried to her side, his hands deft and experienced, before he would allow her to be moved.

Now he spoke reassuringly: 'Nothing to worry about. Shock, perhaps, and bruises. I suggest she goes straight to bed and I'll give her a sedative,' he said curtly.

Lauren struggled to sit up. 'I'm quite all right.' Her eyes filled with tears. 'Oh, Nick, I am so sorry. It was careless of me. I don't know what happened. Did my knee collapse?'

'It's all right, honey child,' Nick said gently, patting her shoulder.

'I can get up,' Lauren insisted. 'I feel . . . fine.' Roland Harvey laid a restraining hand on her shoulder.

'You heard what the doctor said, Lauren. Straight to bed.'

It was not until much later that, remembering the little scene, she realized that it was the first time he had called her by her name.

Now Nick moved swiftly and deftly scooped Lauren up in his arms. 'I'll take her to her room,' he said.

Lauren caught a glimpse of Roland Harvey's angry face, but it was easier to submit than make a scene, so she closed her eyes as they passed groups of people who stared at them curiously.

As Nick laid her on her bed, the tears rolled down her cheeks.

'I'm sorry, Nick,' she said again. 'It's the unforgivable crime, to fall like that.'

He bent over her. 'Don't worry, honey child,' he said gently. 'It can happen to the best of dancers.'

Suddenly his face came closer, and before she could move her head, Nick's mouth was on hers, hard, bruising, ardent . . .

He straightened and backed away as the doctor and Roland Harvey approached the bed. One look at Roland's grim face told Lauren everything.

He had seen Nick kiss her . . . and this time it had, quite definitely, *not* been a brotherly kiss!

# CHAPTER NINE

When she awoke in the morning, Lauren moved her body gingerly, but beyond a little stiffness, she did not feel too bad. She got up, slipped on her blue silk dressing-gown and went to gaze in the mirror. Not much beauty about her today, she thought unhappily. It was strange how soon she looked what her mother called 'peaky'. Perhaps it was the shock of the fall, or the whole day with its various surprises, but she looked very pale.

Girdling the gown tightly round her, she went to stand on the balcony, gazing at the beauty of the cloud-less sky and the green palms silhouetted against the blue water. Why had Nick kissed her like that? He had kissed her before, casually—that time on the sands when he had thanked her. But yesterday he had told her she was beautiful, and then, that same day, had kissed her like that! It made her feel uneasy. No one would ever call Nick a wolf, but it could prove very embarrassing if he started to behave like that . . .

It was all nonsense, she told herself firmly, as she dressed in a canary-yellow sun-suit. She was just leaving her room when the small page came hurrying along with a note.

Immediately she recognized the handwriting. Roland Harvey's! She read it and her heart seemed to sink. He wanted to see her. Immediately.

It must be because of that stupid kiss of Nick's. Why had he to be so silly? Hastily she changed into a coral pink shantung frock and hastily brushed her hair, and then went down to Mr. Harvey's office. Out-side the door she paused, sure she could hear her heart racing, telling herself that she had done nothing wrong, that he could not eat her.

When she went inside, he came to meet her, immaculate in a white tropical suit, his face grave and his eyes concerned. To Lauren's surprise, he took her gently by the hand and led her to the armchair.

'Sit down, Lauren,' he said quietly. 'I want to talk to you.'

She stared at him in surprise. She had come down expecting to have to face his anger, yet here he was, being the kind friendly man she had grown to know and love.

He seated himself behind the wide desk and leaned forward.

'How do you feel?' he asked. 'Not too stiff?'

She shook her head—and inconsistently wished he would not be so kind, for it made her feel all tangled up inside and as if she would cry at any moment. 'I feel fine, thank you,' she answered.

'Why did you fall?' he asked, still gently.

She moved her hands vaguely. 'I don't know. I . . . I . . . All day I had been clumsy, doing silly things. At practice, I couldn't seem to get it right.'

'He should have chosen an easier dance for the evening. He must have seen you were not yourself,' Roland Harvey said sternly.

'He was sure I'd be all right,' Lauren explained quickly. 'He thought I was trying too hard and should relax. I'd been very upset and . . .' She paused, her eyes wide with dismay.

'Lauren,' Roland Harvey said very quietly, 'isn't the situation rather running away with you? I mean, don't you find that you're really too young and inexperienced to cope with this emotional problem? This difficult situation?' He paused, still looking at her anxiously. 'The husband of your best friend . . .'

She felt her cheeks burning. 'But, Mr. Harvey,' she said earnestly, 'you're mistaken. Nick isn't in love with me.'

She hoped she did not sound as desperate as she felt. Nick's kiss had frightened her. Not because it aroused her, for it hadn't, but because of what it might mean.

'I don't blame you in the least,' Roland Harvey continued, ignoring her little outburst. 'You're very young and he is an attractive man. He has a charm, I'm told, that many women find irresistible. I blame him.' His voice hardened.

Lauren was on her feet. 'Please, Mr. Harvey, you must believe me. There's nothing like that, I promise you. Nick loves his wife

150

very much, and—and—you're quite wrong, Nick isn't—he isn't the man I love.' There, she had got it out at last. She stared at him defiantly, only hoping he could not read the truth in her eyes.

'He isn't?' Now Roland Harvey was on his feet, coming to stand in front of her. 'Are you quite sure?' His eyes accused her.

'Quite sure,' she told him, twisting her hands together as she looked up at him. 'That kiss was—was just a kiss. A—a brotherly sort of kiss. He was trying to comfort me because I was crying . . .'

Suddenly Roland Harvey's hands were on her shoulders, his fingers digging into her flesh. Then he bent forward and his mouth lightly brushed hers. 'That's a brotherly kiss. Is that what you mean?' he asked. Before she could answer, he pulled her forward and his arms tightened round her. His mouth came down hard on hers, bruising her lips, pushing her head back.

The room seemed to spin round, and Lauren closed her eyes, feeling herself respond to the kiss, feeling her mouth returning it . . .

He released her abruptly and they stood and stared at one another. 'You see what I mean?' Roland Harvey said harshly. 'That's what a brotherly kiss can lead to . . . something very different.'

Her hand was pressed against her bruised

mouth, her eyes wide and stricken. She was sure he must have felt her response; now he must know her secret. Know that she loved him.

She was shaking. When he told her curtly to sit down, she obeyed gratefully. She kept her eyes down, afraid to face him, afraid to know that he knew the truth.

From behind his desk, he spoke gravely, almost sadly.

'You do see what I mean, Lauren? You must not allow these so-called brotherly kisses. There's no such thing as platonic friendship between men and women. It just doesn't and cannot exist, so don't try that argument.'

'But honestly, Mr. Harvey—' She faced him bravely and went on: 'There isn't anything between us. Nick has only kissed me once. He just isn't that kind of man, and I know he is desperately worried about his wife. She's getting over the operation, but isn't well. I think she misses Nick and . . .'

He lit a cigarette and took his time about doing it, his face intent. Lauren watched him, holding her breath, afraid to say more lest she say the wrong thing.

'Maybe he would be happier if his wife was here,' Roland Harvey said slowly, flicking the dead match into the solid brass ash tray. His eyes never moved as he watched Lauren's face.

She leant forward eagerly, her eyes bright. 'You mean—you mean that she could come here? But she isn't well enough to dance.'

He nodded. 'Naturally I'm aware of that. I meant as a guest of the hotel.'

'Oh, Mr. Harvey, how absolutely wonderful!' Lauren's face was radiant. 'Would you really do that? It would be awfully good of you. Nick will be thrilled.'

'I sincerely hope so,' Roland Harvey said dryly.

Lauren was on her feet. 'You really mean it?'

'I'm not accustomed to saying things I don't mean.'

She blushed. 'I know. I didn't mean . . . I'm so thrilled. Can I go and tell Nick?'

Roland Harvey rose and led the way to the door. 'By all means,' he said smoothly. 'Give him the good news. Tell him that all the necessary arrangements will be made if he simply gives Miss Hunter his home address.'

Lauren found Nick at last in the sunken garden, looking at the tropical fish swimming round under the gold and red waterlilies. How dejected and unhappy he looked, she thought as she hurried to his side, his hands in his pockets, shoulders hunched. Wait until he heard the good news!

'Lauren!' He looked up and came towards her, his face lighting up. 'It's good to see you walking. You sure you're all right?'

She gave him her hands and smiled radiantly at him. 'Nick, I'm fine, and I've got some wonderful news for you. Mr. Harvey says Natalie can come here to stay—to convalesce. Isn't it marvellous of him?'

Nick dropped her hands. 'Natalie? Here?'

Lauren was puzzled. She had expected him to be as excited as she was. More so, in fact. After all, Natalie was his wife, and he was worried about her, and it was very generous of Mr. Harvey.

'Why on earth should Mr. Harvey . . .' Nick began.

Lauren made him sit down with her on one of the stone benches and told him eagerly, if a little uneasily, that she had told Mr. Harvey how worried Nick was about his wife.

'But why did you talk about Natalie?' he asked.

She felt the colour creep into her cheeks. 'He . . . he . . .'

'Saw me kiss you last night?' Nick asked abruptly. 'I'm sorry about that, Lauren. But you looked so sad and so very lovely.'

'I know you didn't mean it,' she told him quickly. 'I told Mr. Harvey that it was just a brotherly kiss.'

'Of course it was,' Nick said, but he gave a strange smile, and suddenly the palms of her hands were damp.

She jumped up. 'Nick, he said if you'll give Miss Hunter your home address, he'll have all the necessary arrangements made to bring Natalie out here. I thought you'd be so pleased,' she finished disconsolately.

Nick managed a smile. 'I am pleased, Lauren. It's wonderful, and will do Natalie a lot of good to get away from the ghastly weather they're having in London, fogs and sleet. It's just . . .' He paused, slowly tracing a pattern on the stone seat with his finger. 'Well, she's going to resent being an invalid and not being able to dance, and I told you she was very jealous.' He sighed. 'She doesn't trust me.'

Lauren took his arm and hugged it. 'Nick, I do, and when I tell her how very well you've behaved out here, I'm sure she will, too. It's just that she loves you so much.'

'I know.' He stood up and smiled at her. 'Thanks, anyhow, honey child. I'll go and see the Hunter now and get things fixed.'

She watched him hurrying towards the hotel and then saw, by her watch, that it was time for the children's dancing class, so she hurried back to the hotel to change. On her way down again, she collected several letters and thrust them into her gay orange and green beach bag.

The children were waiting for her and the time passed swiftly. She thought what a pretty sight it was to see the children of different ages in their gay swimsuits dancing lightly over the sand. She was planning a concert for the parents to see what progress had been made. The only flaw in the lovely morning was the fact that Deborah was not there. Lauren had not seen her since the night when she had stood like a stork and Deborah had recognized her.

After the class, she went to lie in the shade under their favourite palm, feeling comforted, for many of the parents had spoken to her kindly, asking if she was badly bruised from her fall, and saying she should not have bothered to give the dancing class. It was so good to know that many people liked her; to realize that it was only a small minority who thought she had done a disgraceful thing by taking Natalie's place. One thing, Natalie was coming out here, so soon everything would be all right and the gossip would die a natural death.

She settled down to read her letters—one from her parents, one from Natalie, oddly enough, and one from Miss Cartwright. She saved the nicest letter to the last and read Miss Cartwright's first. She had to laugh, for it was so typically Miss Cartwright, congratulating her on holding down a difficult job and pleasing Mr. Harvey.

Miss Cartwright finished:

*'Of course it will take many years of training before you are as polished a dancer as Natalie Natal.'*

That was to make sure that she did not ask for a rise in salary when she got back, Lauren knew. Poor Miss Cartwright—what happiness did she get out of her life, always carefully counting the pennies?

Natalie's letter was full of moans—because she still had pain and the doctors were unsympathetic, because of the terrible weather, and because Nick didn't write often enough. Poor Natalie, Lauren thought as she folded the letter. Well, all her troubles would soon he over and she would be out here, basking in the sun with her beloved Nick.

The parents' letter was lovely and long, for her mother enjoyed letter-writing, and there was a post-script in her father's writing. Everyone was well, Emily had passed her examination, Fleur had started music lessons, and they all thought the famous Roland Harvey was wonderful. He had been very concerned about their daughter's welfare and said she was a marvellous dancer. Then he and Dad had got on like a house on fire and he had wanted to know all about Dad's life as a deep sea diver.

Slowly Lauren folded up the letter. Roland Harvey had made a great impression on the whole family, she thought sadly. How empty the beach seemed without him . . .

Almost as if he had read her thoughts, Roland Harvey was suddenly there by her side, immaculate now in blue Bermuda shorts and a white shirt.

Sitting up quickly, for she always felt at a

disadvantage when sprawled on the hot sands, she looked at him nervously. Now what? He sat down by her side, leaning back on his elbows and putting his dark glasses on.

'Well, was your dancing partner pleased with your good news?'

She felt uncomfortable beneath his stare. 'Of course he was,' she said quickly. Too defiantly? She hoped he would not guess the truth—that Nick had been dismayed.

'Good. Everything is under control. My agent in London will contact Mrs. Natal and make all the necessary arrangements. She can fly out as soon as she likes.' His voice went flat and she glanced at him quickly, but he was not looking at her, he was studying the lighted tip of his cigarette. She looked away immediately, not wanting him to catch her staring at him.

'I've just heard from my family,' she said lightly, wanting to steer the conversation away from Nick. 'You have?' Roland Harvey looked amused. 'I trust they gave a good report of me.'

She turned to him eagerly. 'They all liked you.'

'I'm glad. I liked them. Your mother is a remarkable woman.' His face clouded as he studied his cigarette again. 'I imagine that, in future, you will make exhibition dancing your career? Miss Cartwright implied that she is looking for a suitable partner for you—'

She felt forlorn. Was that the sort of life she

wanted? 'Is she?' she said flatly.

He turned to her and the quick change in his voice made her look up so that their eyes met, frankly, searchingly.

'Lauren, I want to tell—'

Even as he spoke, a small bundle flung herself at them, shouting, 'Miss Woubin!'

'Deborah!' Lauren cried.

Deborah stared at her accusingly. 'You pwomised to see me and you never came. You bwoke your pwomise. You don't love me any more.' Her lower lip trembled.

'I do love you, darling,' Lauren protested. 'And I did want to see you, but . . .' She hesitated, and over Deborah's head her eyes met Roland Harvey's. Should she tell the truth and tell the child that it was Mrs. Lindstrom's fault they had been kept apart?

Roland Harvey spoke gently. 'Deborah, Miss Roubin would have kept her promise to you, but something happened to prevent her.'

Deborah gazed thoughtfully at him, obviously accepted the explanation, and snuggled down between them, holding Lauren's hand firmly in one of her hands, and Roland Harvey's in her other hand, as if afraid they might suddenly vanish.

'Then it's like it used to was?'

Lauren chuckled. 'Yes, darling, it's like it used to was.'

Her eyes exchanged an amused look with Roland Harvey's and, for a moment, she felt very close to him.

Later he told them a comical story of one of his first mountaineering exploits and had them both shaking helplessly with laughter. Then Deborah said proudly that her 'Miss Woubin' was the finest dancer in the world, and Roland Harvey solemnly agreed with her. It was wonderful, Lauren thought, completely relaxed for once.

Shyly, she told him so. 'I'm so very glad you know the truth,' she said. 'I hated living what seemed like a lie.'

He studied her face gravely, but said nothing, and then turned to Deborah. 'Now, young woman,' he said, with a mock sternness that did not deceive the little girl for a moment, for she beamed at him, 'does your mother know you're here?'

Deborah's face grew impish. 'She thinks I'm with Wosie.' She turned to Lauren. 'That's my new nannie, she's awful pwetty, but I don't like her. She never wants to play and can't swim.'

'Rosie is one of the local girls who sometimes acts as nannie to children at the hotel,' Roland Harvey explained briefly. He turned to Deborah. 'So you ran away? Don't you think Rosie will be worried?'

'Oh, no,' Deborah said happily. 'She's talking to her fwiends. She won't think of me until it's time for lunch.'

Lauren watched the quick frown on Roland Harvey's face.

'Is that so?' was all he said, but she imagined he would have something to say to this Rosie about the casual way she performed her duties. He smiled. 'All the same, I think you should run back now in case Rosie reports you as lost. It would frighten your mother and might get you into trouble.' His voice was friendly, with no trace of censure.

'If you say so,' Deborah agreed cheerfully. She looked at Lauren. 'You won't hide from me? You'll be here this afternoon?'

Lauren hesitated and looked at Roland Harvey, who nodded, so she told Deborah she would be there until three o'clock that afternoon.

'We'll swim,' Deborah announced, and stood up. Now it was Roland Harvey's turn. 'You won't forget that you're taking Mummy out to that big ship tonight, will you?' she said sternly. 'She's having her hair done for it and she'll be awful cwoss if you forget.'

The big man ruffled Deborah's hair. 'Of course I won't forget.' He was laughing. 'Have I ever forgotten yet?' He looked at Lauren. 'Some friends of mine have a yacht and are moored off the harbour. They're giving a party tonight.'

She wondered why he bothered to explain. Suddenly she shivered, for it was as if the sun had gone behind a cloud and a chill wind had blown up. She had been so happy, just the three of them. And now she had been reminded of something she had tried to forget—that Roland Harvey and Leila Lindstrom were always together.

Roland Harvey was on his feet, holding out his hand to the child. 'We'll walk back together.' His eyes were grave as he looked at Lauren. 'It will be all right. Deborah will join you later.'

She watched them walk across the sands, the tall, big, impressive man and the small girl dancing gaily by his side, laughing up at him. How they loved one another. What a perfect father he would make.

She turned over on her front and closed her suddenly smarting eyes. The foolish dream was dead. She was sure, now, that Roland Harvey intended to marry Deborah's mother.


## CHAPTER TEN

It was a week before Natalie arrived on the island; a strange week for Lauren, for she felt she was living on borrowed happiness, knowing that it could not last but enjoying it while it did. She lived in a world of dreams, knowing they were simply dreams but enjoying them just the same. Each day, she lay on the sands in the sunshine, while Deborah and Roland Harvey sat with her, talking, laughing, swimming in the warm waters of the lagoon. It was deceptively pleasant, too, in the hotel. Lauren did not know what Roland Harvey could have said to Mrs. Lindstrom, but now, when they met, she was coolly polite. As for Miss Hunter, it seemed to Lauren that she avoided her.

Nick was Lauren's only anxiety. Not that he was difficult or attempted to make love to her. In fact, he was the reverse, for he was very casual, almost offhand at times, seeming to avoid being alone with her, only dancing with her when their duties demanded it. He was choosing the simplest dances for the evening, she noticed. Was it to shorten their practice hours? It was the fact that he was avoiding her that worried her, for she felt that there must be something troubling him.

The day Natalie arrived was the first dull day they had known. The usually cloudless sky was an ominous grey mass, the very sea looked cold and gloomy. The plane came in just after lunch and Lauren went with Nick to meet it. As they waited, they both said how sorry they were that the weather had suddenly changed.

'But it can't last long,' Lauren said optimistically.

Silently they watched the passengers alight, and then Lauren caught her breath with dismay as she recognized Natalie. Was that thin, frail-looking girl the beautiful, glamorous Natalie? She was still lovely with classical features delicately chiselled, her deep blue

163

eyes framed by long dark lashes, but today she looked almost dishevelled, her blonde hair lank, her eyes sunken and lifeless, deep shadows smudged under them, her face gaunt. Usually very elegant, today she looked as if she had flung on her clothes carelessly; they hung loosely on her.

'Nick!' Natalie almost threw herself in his arms. 'At last!' She saw Lauren and her face seemed to go dead, her animation vanishing. 'Hi, Lauren,' she said, and turned back to Nick. 'What's happened to the sunshine, darling?'

'Just hiding behind a cloud,' Nick said cheerfully. 'Have a good trip?'

Sitting silently with them in the car, Lauren wished she had stayed at the hotel and let Nick come on his own, for Natalie was deliberately ignoring her and making her feel awkward.

Lauren had not wanted to come, but Nick had insisted.

'I've told you that Natalie is jealous,' he had said almost irritably. 'If you don't turn up, she'll think we have something to hide, and if you do, she'll hate you for being there—so take your choice,' he had finished, almost churlishly.

Now she was sure she should have stayed behind, and as soon as they reached the hotel, she murmured goodbye and would have slipped away, but Nick stopped her.

'Don't forget,' he said sharply. 'Three

164

o'clock we practise. You were late yesterday.'

Natalie looked at her watch, her mouth sulky. 'Surely you don't have to rehearse every day?' she queried. 'Of course we do,' Nick snapped. 'We do three dances a night and have to ring the changes. There's a lot to be worked out . . . the music, lights . . .'

'We never used to,' Natalie declared, looking at him, with suddenly unhappy eyes.

Nick looked annoyed. 'We never danced at the Island Hotel, Paradise Island,' he snapped. 'Three o'clock, Lauren, and on the dot.'

Lauren escaped from them gladly and hurried to her room. She shivered a little, partly because of the dull day, partly because already she had sensed tension between Nick and Natalie.

Had Natalie always been difficult? Lauren looked back and realized that although they had been friends for a long time, she really knew Natalie hardly at all. They had never had long talks or been alone together. At the Cartwright School of Dancing, Natalie had been one of the star dancers, and although she was always friendly with Lauren, they had little in common. Natalie disliked children and could not understand Lauren's enthusiasm for her classes. At their flat, Natalie had always been the perfect hostess, sympathetic, witty, but always passing on to the next guest.

So really, Lauren realized, she did not know Natalie at all. Now Lauren began to remember other things. Nick congratulating her on not grumbling about the tiring practices, and he had said once that it was a pity Natalie was so lazy, that she thought beauty was enough, but in these days of highly competitive living, beauty came a long way behind personality and perseverance.

It was as if that first day set the keynote to everything. Nothing pleased Natalie, not even when, a few days later, the threatened storm vanished and the sun shone again out of a clear blue sky. Nothing was right. No, she did not want to sit on the sands and sunbathe, her skin was too sensitive; yet, several times, Lauren saw Natalie walking along the family beach, looking intently at the couples or groups, looking towards Lauren where she sat with Deborah. Not even a trip round the island interested her, and only the sight of the graceful yacht, moored in the harbour, seemed to bring her to life.

'Now if only we could have a yacht like that,' she said enviously.

'What would you do with it, if we had one?' Nick asked bluntly. 'You're always sea-sick.'

In the old days, Natalie would have laughed and parried it with a joke, but that day, her eyes swelled with tears and she looked reproachfully at Nick.

'Shall we ever be rich, Nick?' she asked.

Nick frowned. 'We'll have to work for it.' He turned away. 'I don't think I'm doing too

166

badly.'

Lauren grew more and more uncomfortable as the days became weeks. Everything now was different. Poor Natalie seemed to have tarnished the gloss and spoiled things for them all.

One night Natalie had been particularly difficult, and after the dancing was over Lauren slipped away from the crowded ballroom and went to stand on the wide veranda. It was deserted, and she leaned over the stone parapet. It was a perfect night, a night for romance, for joy. The water in the lagoon was absolutely still, slashed by the golden pathway of the moonlight. Even the palms were still, as if holding their breath expectantly. Something was going to happen . . .

It had to happen, Lauren thought unhappily, gripping the wall. How long could she stand the strain? Everything she did or said was wrong, according to Natalie. It was growing so bad that now Lauren thought cautiously before she spoke, and even so, she was always saying the wrong thing. Natalie insisted on watching every practice, criticized Lauren's dancing, the way she wore the lovely gowns that should have been Natalie's, and she was always asking questions about Nick and his pupils. It was a jealous, querulous Natalie who distorted every innocent remark, who was forever watching, as if waiting to pounce.

Only that evening when Nick had been alone for a moment with Lauren, he said angrily that he wished she had minded her own business and had never suggested to Mr. Harvey that Natalie joined them.

'You think things are difficult,' he had said crossly, 'but you have no idea what I suffer. She knows I earn extra money by giving dancing lessons, but the way she creates, you'd think I do it for fun. She always was possessive and jealous—but now, well, she's the end!'

It would have been no good to point out to Nick, in the mood he was in, that it had not been her idea to suggest Natalie came out to them, Lauren thought miserably. Nor that if Nick had not kissed her, Mr. Harvey would never have suggested it.

Now as she stared blindly at the beauty, she found herself wishing that she had never come to Paradise Island. If it meant wrecking Nick's happy marriage, it was too big a price to pay for a few weeks of happiness. All that happiness had gone, killed by Natalie's probing jealousy. Lauren had seen her talking to Miss Hunter and even to Mrs. Lindstrom, and Lauren had wondered what tales those two women had told her.

What a long tiring day it had been, Lauren thought, aching with heartache and weariness. It had begun that very morning when she missed Deborah from the dancing class and had known that it probably meant that Roland

Harvey had taken Deborah and her mother out for the day. That had hurt, foolishly of course, but still it always hurt to think of Roland Harvey with Mrs. Lindstrom.

Later, as she lay under the palm tree, Lauren had been shocked and startled when Deborah had come stumbling across the sands, white-faced, tearful, clinging to her tightly, but refusing to say what was wrong. Lauren had been so worried when Deborah's tearful trembling continued that she had taken her back to the hotel and found the hotel doctor, who was busy and not too pleased about being disturbed.

'There's nothing wrong with the child,' he had grunted. 'Must have had a fright of some kind. Put her to bed and give her these tablets. They'll make her sleep, and in the morning she'll have forgotten all about it.'

Lauren had hesitated before taking Deborah to the small bedroom that led off her mother's magnificent bedroom. Ought she to find and tell Mrs. Lindstrom? But when she suggested this to Deborah, the child burst into hysterical tears and clung to her, begging her not to tell her mother. In the end, Lauren took the child to her bedroom, tucked her up in bed, gave her the tablets, and sat by her side until the child was sound asleep. Then, very quietly, because it was nearly time for dance practice, Lauren had crept out of the room. Closing the bedroom door softly, she jumped with surprise as she saw Roland Harvey walking down the corridor towards her.

'What on earth' he began, looking down at her, a slight frown on his rugged face.

Lauren was not listening, she was too worried. 'Mr. Harvey, have you seen Deborah's mother?' she asked. He looked puzzled. 'I think she's playing bridge, but I'm not sure.'

'Well, you see . . .' Lauren started to tell him when a page came darting down the corridor, a note on a silver platter in his hand, and Roland Harvey turned to look at him.

Lauren hesitated, but he seemed to have forgotten her, tearing the envelope open with a quick decisive movement. After all, was there any need to alarm him? The doctor had said it was nothing. And would Mrs. Lindstrom really be interested? That was an unkind thought, but . . . Lauren saw the time on her watch and caught her breath with dismay. She must not be late or Natalie would swoop on that as an excuse to give her a lecture.

So she had rushed off to the ballroom and found Natalie sitting, arms folded, eyes sharp, and Nick angry.

'You're late,' Nick snapped. 'This is getting to be a habit.'

'I'm sorry,' Lauren apologized. 'Deborah wasn't very well, so I had to see the doctor about her and then put her to bed.'

'Of all the feeble excuses!' Nick's face was

red, he looked as if about to explode with anger. Uneasily Lauren realized that he and Natalie had been quarrelling again; when he picked on her, it was always a sign of that.

The practice went smoothly, although Lauren felt a little faint and dizzy, and then realized that she had eaten no lunch. Fortunately her trip to the hairdresser did not take long as they were demonstrating modern ballroom dances only that evening and Nick had said she could be herself, Lauren Roubin.

In her bedroom, Lauren had sent for sandwiches and coffee and had worried about Deborah. Then, seeing some magazines she had been lent by one of the guests and knowing how Natalie loved the glossy, expensive monthlies, she gathered up an armful and decided to take them to Natalie; it might help to put her in a better mood. On the way, she looked in on Deborah and saw the child was sound asleep, sprawled across the bed, completely relaxed, looking like a little angel. Lauren had straightened the sheet, lightly dropped a kiss on Deborah's flushed cheek and tiptoed away. She was sure there was no cause to worry; the doctor had said it was nothing, that a good sleep would put things right.

Natalie was alone, in a deep armchair, curled up. She looked up with hostile eyes. 'What do you want?' she demanded.

Lauren hesitated. 'I thought you might like

171

these magazines.'

'Thanks. Sit down, I'm bored to tears,' Natalie said. 'I thought you were with Nick.' She looked at Lauren sharply, eyes bright with suspicion.

Lauren stifled a sigh. 'I've been to the hairdresser and—and then came here.'

She watched Natalie and thought that despite her unhappiness and discontent, the rest, good food and sunshine had done her good. Natalie looked a different person. If only her mouth didn't droop so miserably and she wasn't always so difficult! Lauren suddenly noticed that Natalie was playing with a necklace of some lovely tawny-coloured stones. It looked vaguely familiar to Lauren, but knowing Natalie's habit of jumping on her no matter what she said, she decided not to mention the necklace. Was it a peace-offering from Nick? Maybe she had seen the necklace in the hotel *boutique*, which sold fabulously lovely things.

'Any interesting news?' Natalie asked in a bored voice, handling the necklace, twisting it round her arm, holding it up to the light. Lauren wondered uneasily if Natalie was deliberately trying to attract her attention with the necklace; perhaps she wanted her to mention it?

'I'm afraid not,' Lauren said nervously. It was like walking on hot tiles talking to this new Natalie. She racked her brain for something innocent to say. 'I looked in to see how Deborah was, but she's still asleep.'

'Deborah? That precocious brat! You're wasting your time smarming over her. It won't get you anywhere.'

Lauren flushed, both because of the implication of Natalie's words, and the ugly voice she had used. 'I'm very fond of Deborah,' she said firmly.

Natalie looked at her with raised eyebrows. 'Are you, indeed? Quite sure it's not Mr. Harvey you're very fond of, Lauren? That's the tale that's going round, and you're making a laughing-stock of yourself, the way you play up to him. You're just wasting time. Mrs. Lindstrom has got him nicely snaffled.' She laughed.

Lauren was on her feet. 'I am not chasing Mr. Harvey!' she snapped.

The door had opened and Nick was there, scowling at them.

'For Pete's sake, can a man get no peace? What are you two fighting about now?' he demanded, leaning against the wall, a tall handsome man with weary eyes.

'We weren't fighting, darling,' Natalie said sweetly. 'I was just advising Lauren to give up hope where the great Roland is concerned. She hasn't an earthly.'

Nick was not listening. His face was furious as he strode across the room. 'Where did you get that?' he demanded harshly as he grabbed her arm and held it up so that he could see the necklace twisted round it.

Natalie was laughing at him. 'Wouldn't you like to know?'

Lauren had seized her chance and slipped quietly out of the room, back to her own room and a bath. So Nick had not bought Natalie that lovely necklace? Then who had?

All through their three exhibition dances that night, Nick had been very silent, and this had been her first opportunity to slip away from the glare and noise and escape out here to the peaceful beauty of the night. She wondered how she could go on bearing the strain of the unpleasant atmosphere and the quarrels. What should she do? If only Natalie were strong enough to take her proper place as Nick's partner! In that moment of despair, Lauren felt she would have gladly left the island.

'Is there something wrong?' a deep, well-known, well-loved voice asked quietly.

Lauren jumped nervously and turned to the tall man who had approached noiselessly. She stared up into his impassive face, thinking, with a sickening lurch of her heart, that she did not know if she would have the strength enough voluntarily to leave this beautiful island and the chance to see this man.

'Oh, Mr. Harvey, I didn't hear you.'

'You were miles away,' he told her. How strong and safe he looked, in his well-cut dinner jacket and trousers, his hair so smooth.

'What were you thinking about?' he asked. 'Has something upset you?'

It was the kindness in his voice that was her undoing. What if it was the sort of voice you use to a child, it was still compassionate, sympathetic.

She felt the tears filling her eyes and she could not stop them. She stared up at him blindly, the tears hovering on her long curling lashes, her mouth trembling. 'It's just . . . just everything,' she whispered.

He gave her his handkerchief, put his arm round her shoulders, and led her away from the long french windows that led into the ballroom. He only stopped when they reached the quiet part of the veranda outside the closed windows of his office. Then he made her sit down on one of the long comfortable seats and took hold of both her hands, looking down at her.

'Tell me all about it,' he said.

Somehow the words tumbled out. 'Everything I do is wrong. Natalie used not to be like this. She was so kind, such fun, but now . . . now she says that I dance clumsily, that I don't wear the beautiful dresses properly, that I'm—I'm—' Lauren stopped herself just in time, staring up at the silent man with horror in her eyes. How nearly she had told him that now Natalie was saying that she was chasing him! If she had gone on and said that! She shivered.

'Lauren,' Roland Harvey said very quietly in the voice of a sympathetic adult to a child. 'Try to see the situation through Natalie's eyes.'

Startled, she stopped crying. Whatever she had expected him to say, it had not been this. He was defending Natalie!

'Through her eyes?' she echoed.

Roland Harvey released her hands and sat back, folding his arms and half smiling. 'Yes, through Natalie's eyes.' Very slowly, with maddening precision, he lighted two cigarettes and gave her one. 'I don't think you often smoke, but this may calm you down a little,' he said. 'I want you to realize that in the first place, Natalie is suffering from post-operative blues. She feels weak and is worried because she feels she should be stronger by now. Secondly, this booking was just as important to Natalie as to her husband, and she has the feeling that she has let her husband down. Thirdly, she is, I gather, a naturally jealous and possessive woman.'

He flicked the ash off his cigarette and looked at the silent girl by his side, sitting so tensely, staring at him.

'Now what have we to consider?' he went on slowly. 'She comes out to this beautiful place, delighted at the thought of a restful holiday that will cost them nothing, glad to join her beloved husband, and what does she find? Her place has been most successfully taken by a very lovely and talented girl. Think, Lauren, she must be in her mid-thirties. She probably resents your youth, your beauty and your talent. It's understandable. Nick quite obviously enjoys dancing with you. Imagine how you would feel in Natalie's place. Wouldn't you see yourself as a rival . . . perhaps a successor? She may even feel that her wonderful life as Nick's dancing partner is over, that you will be his partner in future.'

'Nick would never—' Lauren began indignantly.

'Wouldn't he?' Roland Harvey asked dryly. 'If Miss Cartwright said so? If it paid him? The two of you together make an excellent team. You're malleable, quick to learn, eager to please and a very much easier partner than a spoilt, fretful wife.'

'I'm sure you're wrong,' Lauren said. Unconsciously she twisted her hands together, staring at him in dismay. 'I see what you mean about Natalie. I hadn't thought of it like that, but . . . but really, really, Nick wouldn't—'

'I'm not saying that Nick does feel like that,' Roland Harvey pointed out quietly. 'I'm merely trying to show you how it might appear to Natalie.'

'But I wouldn't . . . Natalie must know . . .'

'Look, Lauren, I'm afraid we all have a tendency to judge others by the way we would behave ourselves. You wouldn't expect a girl to behave like that because, to you, such behaviour would be disloyal. But I imagine that Natalie, in a similar situation, would not scruple to steal a man as a dancing partner, or as a husband, if she loved him.'

'Natalie wouldn't,' Lauren said, shocked. 'She's a very good person.'

'I wonder. I don't say she is immoral—probably amoral. She would say it's a case for the survival of the fittest. That remark has often been used to cover quite incredible actions.' He stubbed out his cigarette with a quick impatient movement. 'You are—though I'm aware you don't like to be reminded of it—very young and naive, Lauren. You believe that people are automatically good whereas, unfortunately, few of us are. Most of us do things we are secretly ashamed of doing.'

Lauren stared at him. 'I'm sure you don't,' she said.

He smiled, his eyes crinkling at the corners. 'Thank you, Lauren. I wish I could be as sure.' There was a pause while they stared at one another. 'You know, Lauren,' he said softly, 'I can't blame Natalie for being jealous. You're so very lovely.'

'I am?' She stared at him dazed, her hand flying to the pearls round her throat.

Suddenly his hand closed over hers. It was warm and she caught her breath, as she still stared at him.

'Lauren,' he said, his voice low, 'who is this man you love? Are you sure you love him?'

178

The quick staccato tap-tap of high heels sounded clearly, and Roland Harvey dropped Lauren's hand and stood up, facing the corner of the balcony round which the wearer of the shoes would appear. Lauren stood by his side, slim, ethereal-looking in her diaphanous chiffon gown of palest green. In a moment, Leila Lindstrom appeared in view, exquisitely dressed in a black gown, with diamonds blazing at her neck and wrist. As she saw them, she faltered, looking surprised.

'They told me you were out here, Roland. I thought you were alone.' She shot Lauren a glance of hostility. 'It's very urgent,' she finished, and sounded agitated.

'In a few moments, Leila,' Roland Harvey said quietly. He took a key from his pocket and unlocked the french window, opening it, turning on a light. 'Please sit down, Leila. I'll be with you in a moment.'

Mrs. Lindstrom walked past Lauren and sat down, and Roland Harvey closed the door.

'I'll see you to your room,' he said curtly to the silent girl. 'You'll feel better in the morning.'

'You needn't,' she said. 'I can—'

'I'm aware of that, but I want to see you to your room,' he said coldly. His hand closed over her arm and she shivered. What had happened? Why had Mrs. Lindstrom's appearance so altered his mood?

She had almost to run to keep up with his

long strides.

Outside her bedroom door, he paused and looked down at her. His voice had changed again; once more it was kind, gentle.

'Don't let it worry you too much, Lauren. I'm sure it's simply because Natalie is still far from well. We'll try to think of something.' He stared down into her upturned face. 'You may be interested to know,' he said slowly, 'that I've decided to sell the hotel.'

'You have?' She found it hard to breathe. 'You're going to climb another mountain?'

He smiled. 'Something like that, I suppose. I seem to be always searching for something, but I'm not quite sure what it is.'

He took the key from her hand and unlocked the door, opening it and standing to one side to let her enter. But as she began to move, Lauren was frozen into stillness.

The room was not empty. Miss Hunter sat on one chair, her eyes bright, while on another sat Mr. Dixie, the hotel detective.

On the small table lay an amber-coloured, tawny golden-brown necklace—the necklace she had seen Natalie playing with that day.

'Ah, at last, Miss Roubin!' Miss Hunter said, rising and coming towards them, her eyes glinting. She looked at Roland Harvey.

'I'm very sorry about this, Mr. Harvey, but when Mrs. Lindstrom reported the theft of her jewels and Miss Roubin had been seen leaving Mrs. Lindstrom's bedroom this afternoon, I took the liberty of having her room searched. We found these,' she finished dramatically, pointing at the necklace.

'Are they Mrs. Lindstrom's?' Lauren gasped.

'Of course.' Roland Harvey's voice was tart. 'You must have seen her wearing them.'

Lauren looked up at him, her eyes bewildered. 'I wondered whose they were. They looked familiar. I thought—'

She stopped herself, feeling the hot guilty colour flood her cheeks as she met his unblinking stare. Had Natalie stolen them, then hidden them here to involve her?

'I didn't steal them, Mr. Harvey,' she said slowly. 'I don't know how they can have got into my room.'

She wondered why he didn't speak to her, reassure her, why he kept staring at her in that strange way.

Suddenly she was frightened. 'I didn't steal them. I didn't. You can't think I'm a thief?'

'But I did see you coming out of Mrs. Lindstrom's room. What were you doing there?' he asked, his voice distant.

Her hand flew to her throat nervously. 'I can explain . . .'

Miss Hunter's laugh was ugly, triumphant. 'Of course you can. You'll have an explanation—you'll probably say that Deborah was ill and you had to put her to bed.'

Lauren swung round to stare at her in

disbelief. 'But that is what happened,' she said.

Miss Hunter smiled smugly. 'It was very clever of you to work out such a story. Very shrewd. But, Miss Roubin, you *are* shrewd, and cunning, too. You even asked the doctor to examine her and persuaded him to give you some tablets to make the child sleep.'

'I did take her to the doctor, he did give me some.' Bewildered, trapped, Lauren looked from one face to another. On the detective's face she saw quick sympathy that vanished almost instantly. 'You must believe me, Mr. Harvey. Deborah was badly frightened about something. She came running to me and—'

'Then why didn't you tell me about Deborah when I saw you this afternoon coming out of her mother's room?' he asked coldly.

Lauren twisted her hands together. 'I was going to . . . then the page boy brought you that note, and . . . and . . . I didn't think Deborah could be really ill as the doctor hadn't seemed to think so, and I was late already for my practice and—'

'A likely story,' Miss Hunter sneered. 'A clever little tale you rigged up. Very clever, but not quite clever enough, Miss Roubin.'

Lauren was not listening to her. She was staring at the big, handsome man whose face was so stern.

She felt as if her heart was breaking. 'Mr. Harvey,' she said once more, desperately, 'you do believe me? You can't believe that I'm a thief?'

# CHAPTER ELEVEN

Would she ever forget that moment? He had turned away, as if he wanted to waste no more time on her. His voice was cold as he said: 'It's late—someone is waiting to see me, so we will continue this discussion in the morning . . .'

Could she ever forget Miss Hunter's instant: 'There's nothing to discuss, Mr. Harvey. We've caught the girl red-handed.'

Or Roland Harvey's controlled voice as he repeated: 'I said we will discuss this in the morning, Miss Hunter.'

Miss Hunter had gone close to him, putting out a hand to touch his arm. 'But, Mr. Harvey . . . I'm afraid it's my fault. I should have seen through the girl at once and—'

'Miss Hunter!' Roland Harvey had roared. Lauren caught her breath—it was the first time she had heard him raise his voice in anger. She could see that he was very angry indeed. 'I said we will continue this in the morning. Are you deaf?'

He went to the table, scooped up the necklace, and said: 'I shall return these to their rightful owner. Now if you will kindly leave . . .'

Lauren stood very still, eyes tightly shut. She

183

could not bear to meet Miss Hunter's triumphant gaze any longer or the quick unhappy look Mr. Dixie, the friendly detective, had. She heard the door open and opened her eyes, seeing Roland Harvey by the door, waiting for Miss Hunter and Mr. Dixie to go through. Then he turned and looked at Lauren, who stared at him silently, hugging herself unhappily.

'Don't worry, Lauren,' he said gently. 'Sleep well. We'll sort this out tomorrow. Goodnight.'

And with that he left the room, closing the door behind him. Lauren felt the hysterical laughter bubbling out of her throat and then spilling itself in tears as she flung herself on the bed and sobbed. It was not being accused that hurt; it was the look on Roland Harvey's face, the sad, disillusioned note in his voice as he told her not to worry. He believed she was a thief. He had been sad—the same sadness he would have felt if small Deborah had done something naughty. It was the sort of voice that parents use, often unintentionally, as a weapon with which to punish their children, that hurt disillusionment that is more powerful than any brief spanking could be.

She washed her face and tried to think sensibly.

First of all, why hadn't she recognized the jewels at once as belonging to Mrs. Lindstrom? She had often seen them before. Secondly, how had Natalie got hold of them?

Had she stolen them, would she have flaunted them like that? And Nick? Nick had recognized them instantly. Lauren could remember the surprise in his harsh voice as he demanded to be told where Natalie had got them, and Natalie had laughed teasingly. Thirdly, if Natalie had the jewels, then how had they got up here, in her bedroom? Lauren wondered. Could Natalie have hidden them here and then hinted to Miss Hunter? Were they in this together, perhaps?

Yet it was hard to imagine Natalie doing a terrible thing like that. Besides, Nick had seen her with the jewels . . .

Lauren felt trapped. How quick Miss Hunter had been to destroy what she called a 'so-called excuse'. How had she known about Deborah's visit to the doctor? Unless the doctor had grumbled to her about being disturbed for nothing . . . or Mr. Dixie had seen her come out of the bedroom, and when it was reported that the valuable necklace was missing, had put two and two together. It did look bad, no denying it, Lauren thought miserably, as she paced up and down the room. But once again, it all came back to the terrible truth—Roland Harvey did not trust her. He had been able to doubt her word. He thought she was a thief.

In the end, she went to bed—to toss and turn, to weep a little, to try to tell herself that Roland Harvey was a just man and tomorrow he would give her a hearing. At last she slept.

She awoke early and felt and looked a complete wreck, she decided, looking in the mirror at the pale girl with swollen red eyes, rumpled hair, drooping mouth. It was not yet seven o'clock, but she felt she must get out of the hotel—walk along the sands alone, perhaps. She showered and dressed, choosing a simple blue frock, twisting her lank hair into a pony-tail, not bothering what she looked like, wondering how she was going to face Miss Hunter's accusation and Roland Harvey's cold disillusioned eyes without bursting into tears.

The door handle turned and she swung round, instantly on the defensive, for there was only one person in the hotel who would walk into her room without knocking.

Like an animal at bay, Lauren faced Miss Hunter across the room. Miss Hunter looked amused, her eyes triumphant, as she stood there, elegant in grey silk. She closed the door behind her and came into the room.

'Miss Roubin,' her voice was very formal, 'Mr. Harvey wishes me to handle this unpleasant matter with the minimum of fuss. The jewels have been returned and Mrs. Lindstrom has been persuaded to make no charge against you. Mr. Harvey wishes you to leave immediately. Kindly pack at once. I'm afraid I cannot let you have Claudia to help you, as Mr. Harvey's express orders are that you are to speak to no one in the hotel—no member of the staff nor any guest in the hotel.'

Lauren managed to break the spell and move. 'But Mr. Harvey can't . . . he said we would discuss . . .' Her voice faltered and stopped because of Miss Hunter's amused scorn. Then she found fresh courage. This was not the way a man like Roland Harvey would behave. 'I should have the right to—'

'Defend yourself?' Miss Hunter smiled. 'You condemned yourself last night. You admitted you recognized the jewels, confessed to a carefully-arranged story. Naturally Mr. Harvey is very vexed because you dragged Mrs. Lindstrom's child into it.'

'I did not drag her,' Lauren said indignantly. 'She was hysterical, very frightened.'

'I daresay she was frightened. It would have been quite simple for you to tell her an alarming story or even to push her over to make her show some signs of an upset. It was a mistake to take Mrs. Lindstrom's jewels, Miss Roubin. She happens to be a very special friend of Mr. Harvey's.' Miss Hunter's mouth twisted in an ugly fashion.

Lauren closed her eyes. Need Miss Hunter remind her of that? Then her just, natural anger returned. No one had the right to accept her guilt as a fact without giving her a chance.

'I insist on seeing Mr. Harvey,' she said.

Miss Hunter shook her head. 'Mr. Harvey doesn't want to see you. You should count yourself lucky that he's being so generous about this. He is giving you a chance to slip away quietly before anyone hears about it. You're to take the plane that leaves at nine o'clock. He will naturally have to write and explain to Miss Cartwright what has happened.'

Lauren suddenly felt exhausted, as if she had been battered about. It was like banging your head on a brick wall.

'Who—who will dance?' she wanted to know.

Miss Hunter smiled. 'Natalie declares that she is strong enough. Naturally she is delighted to have you go, so that she can have her husband back again.'

Lauren turned to stare blindly out of the open window. What should she do? What could she do? She could make a scene and refuse to go—tell Mr. Harvey that she had seen Natalie with the jewels. But would he believe her? If he did, it would mean terrible trouble for Nick—probably ruin their future, might even finish their marriage. Was it worth it? She did not mind what people said or thought. The cruellest cut of all was that Roland Harvey believed her guilty.

'All right. I'll go on the plane,' she said.

'That's the first sensible thing you've said for a long time,' Miss Hunter said briskly. 'You must go down the back way and the car will be waiting. Naturally you will remember to take only your own clothes.'

Lauren turned round angrily. 'Naturally!'

Miss Hunter's eyes were flashing. 'I only wondered, as you seem to find it difficult to differentiate between your property and other people's. Jewels . . . husbands . . . so why shouldn't you be in the same predicament where clothes are concerned?'

'Miss Hunter ' Lauren began indignantly, and then stopped. She was horribly near tears, and whatever happened, this awful woman must not see her crying.

Miss Hunter turned to the door. 'Remember you are to speak to no one. Particularly not Deborah, Mr. Harvey said.' She closed the door behind her, and for a long moment Lauren stood there, her hands to her smarting eyes, fighting back the tears. Then she tried to make her anger overcome the pain. Mr. Harvey was treating her very badly. Everyone was innocent until proved guilty— and she had not been proved guilty. She had a right . . .

She felt horribly alone—as if everyone was her enemy. To whom could she turn? Roland Harvey had obviously washed his hands of her. He believed her guilty of theft. Nick? Yet if Natalie had planted the necklace here, mustn't Nick have been involved? It seemed hard to believe, but . . .

She swept her hair out of her eyes and went to the wardrobe, angrily flinging her own clothes on to the bed, not looking at the lovely gowns and silk suits that would now be Natalie's. Natalie had won. Well, if it made her any happier, or made Nick happier, it would be one good thing saved from this chaos of her love.

Chaos of my love . . . She repeated the words over and over again, trying to keep from thinking, from realizing the truth. That Roland believed her guilty . . .

She caught a glimpse of her bedside clock and realized she had very little time left if she was to keep to the routine Roland Harvey had ordered. She had been banished from Paradise . . . the chaos of my love . . . Half crying, half laughing, she told herself she might even end up as a song-writer. She hurried to the wash basin and dipped her burning face into cold water, again and again, trying to calm down. She must leave with dignity.

She swallowed unhappily. Was she doing right by meekly agreeing to this monstrous solution—if solution it could be called? Obviously all Roland Harvey cared about was the reputation of the hotel. Perhaps this was Mrs. Lindstrom's condition, perhaps she had threatened otherwise to make a charge against her.

At last she had packed her two suitcases with her own clothes. She had no coat, but that could not be helped. The thick white coat she had worn on the flight out had been part of the Natalie Natal wardrobe. She shivered suddenly, imagining Miss Cartwright's anger. And what would her family say? Her father would be furious—he would want to see Roland Harvey, want to fight it. What was she to do?

She saw no one as she left her room and hurried down the discreet back stairs and through the side door. There was a car waiting for her. The chauffeur glanced up, slid out of his seat, and took her cases. In a few moments, the car was starting to go down the winding circular drive. Lauren gave one last look at the hotel.

Racing across the lawn towards her, waving and shouting frantically, came Nick.

'Please drive fast,' Lauren said to the driver, leaning forward in her seat.

She looked away from Nick, her teeth biting painfully into her lower lip. Roland Harvey had said she was to speak to no one. She would obey him for the last time.

The last time . . . She slumped back in her seat, realizing what that meant.

As the car swooped along the winding drive, Lauren saw that Nick was racing across the smooth green lawn, planning to get to the gate and cut them off.

'Hurry! Hurry!' she urged the chauffeur. She knew suddenly that she wanted to talk to no one. No one at all.

But she was left with no choice, for Nick reached the gates and swung them shut, leaning against them, his arms outstretched. He was panting and obviously trying to get his breath back as the chauffeur slammed on the brakes and came to a halt, sitting still with his dark face impassive, as if well used to the strange behaviour of white people.

'Lauren,' Nick said, coming to the car, leaning on the door, glaring at her, 'what's the big idea, walking out on me like this?'

She saw his face mistily. 'Nick, I'm not . . . It isn't that . . .'

'Then what is it?'

'Nick, please! I can't talk about it. I've got to catch the plane. Mr. Harvey said so. Please, Nick . . .' Her voice was trembling.

Nick jerked the door of the car open and told her curtly to move over. 'Let's get this straight. Mr. Harvey said you were to catch the plane?'

'Yes, Nick, I've got to go.' Lauren sounded desperate.

Nick looked grim. 'Oh, no, you don't, my girl, not without a proper explanation.' He turned to the chauffeur. 'Turn round and take us back to the hotel,' he ordered.

The chauffeur stared at him and, still with no change of expression on his dark face, obeyed, slowly reversing the car.

'Nick, Mr. Harvey said—' Lauren caught the sleeve of his thin jacket.

'I don't give a damn what Mr. Harvey said,' Nick told her. 'You're my partner, and you

192

can't do this. He can say it to my face and then we'll all leave together. He has no right . . .' Nick was breathing heavily, his face angry. He made an effort to calm down and his voice was quieter as he asked Lauren to explain. 'You'd better brief me quickly before we see the great man. What led up to this?'

Lauren folded her hands together tightly, her eyes on Nick's face, as she tried to sort out her jumbled memories and put them concisely into shape. 'Last night I was upset, Nick, and Mr. Harvey found me on the veranda and we talked. Mrs. Lindstrom came and said she must see him urgently, and he put her in his office and insisted on seeing me to my room.'

She spoke rapidly, for the car was approaching the hotel. 'We—well, when we opened the door Miss Hunter was waiting for me and . . . and Mr. Dixie, and they accused me of stealing Mrs. Lindstrom's topaz necklace. They said they found it in my room and Mr. Harvey had seen me leaving Mrs. Lindstrom's bedroom. I told you about taking Deborah to the doctor? Well, Miss Hunter knew all about that, she said it was a story I had invented, but, Nick, Deborah really was frightened about something . . .'

The car stopped outside the hotel. Nick opened the car door and helped Lauren out. He looked even more angry than he had before, but his voice was controlled and he smiled at her.

'Go straight to your room and lock the door. Don't open it until I come for you.'

'Nick, where are you going?' She clung to his arm, staring at him fearfully.

'To see Mr. Harvey, of course.'

'He's furious with me.' Lauren's voice was unsteady.

'I'm furious with him!' Nick bit the words off angrily. 'When did you see him? Where?'

'Last night, I told you.'

Nick frowned. 'I mean this morning. Or did he tell you last night that you were to clear out?'

Lauren looked at him. This was a new Nick—stern, strong, his anger well under control. 'Last night he said we would continue this—the discussion, rather—this morning.'

'And this morning?'

Lauren twisted her fingers together. People were beginning to stroll by them, glancing curiously in their direction.

'Nick, I didn't see him this morning. He sent Miss Hunter. She gave me his message.'

'Go on.'

Quickly Lauren repeated the whole conversation, and he did not interrupt her once. When she had finished, he merely said: 'Go to your room, honey child, and stop worrying. I'll have coffee and sandwiches sent up, for I bet you missed out on your breakfast. Do something to your face and wait for me. One last thing . . .' He held her arm tightly for a moment and looked stern, 'Promise you won't walk out on me?'

She looked up into his lean, kind face and knew that she trusted him completely. None of it made sense, but she was quite sure that Nick was her friend.

'I promise, Nick.'

'Good girl!'

He walked with her to the lift, and when she reached her own room, she locked the door, hastily washing her face and making up. The coffee came with crisp rolls and butter, and after the silent waiter had left the tray with her, Lauren locked the door again. She was sure she could not eat anything, but she was surprised to find that she enjoyed the meal and felt better afterwards.

She sat on the balcony, looking at the lagoon and the waving palms, and felt a strange serenity. Nick had said everything would be all right. Soon Roland Harvey would know the truth—that she was not a thief.

Like a knife stabbing her in the heart, the pain shot through her. He believed she was a thief.

The loud knock on the door made her jump. 'It's only me—Nick,' he called.

She hurried to open it. He still looked stern and yet, at the same time, looked very pleased about something. He gave her a quick searching look and nodded as if satisfied.

'Good girl. You look more yourself now.

Come on.'

'Is Mr. Harvey very angry?' Lauren asked nervously.

'Yes,' Nick said slowly, taking her arm. 'He is angry, but not with you.'

'Not with me?' she echoed.

Then who could he be angry with? Had he discovered that Natalie had put the necklace in her room? If Natalie had, that was—or had Nick told him? Yet Nick was so cheerful. The thoughts milled round in her mind and nothing made sense, but Nick gave her no chance to ask questions as he hurried her to Mr. Harvey's office.

The room seemed to be empty until Roland Harvey moved out of the shadows and stood in the sunshine that came through the open windows. His dark red hair gleamed. He looked very impressive in his well-cut suit, tall, broad-shouldered, stern.

'Please sit down, Miss Roubin,' he said formally, and turned to Nick. 'Would you tell Miss Hunter I'm ready to see her?'

Alone in the room with Roland Harvey, Lauren looked up worriedly at the tall good-looking man who came to stand by her, looking down at her so gravely. 'You are feeling better today?' he asked.

She swallowed. 'Better?'

He nodded. 'You were very emotionally disturbed last night. That's why I postponed the inquiry.'

Her hand flew to her throat. 'You believe I'm a thief,' she accused him in an unsteady voice, just as the door opened and Miss Hunter stalked in, followed by Nick.

For a moment it was as if Miss Hunter faltered when she saw Lauren, but in a moment she had gained her composure and came right into the room, her tight thin mouth the only sign of her temporary disturbance.

'You wanted to see me, Mr. Harvey?' Her voice was cool and confident. 'I'm very busy just now and—'

Roland Harvey sat down behind the desk. His voice curt, he said: 'Yes, I do, Miss Hunter. Please sit down, both of you.'

In silence they obeyed. Miss Hunter sat very upright, her hands folded on her lap. She avoided looking in Lauren's direction.

Roland Harvey began quietly: 'I understand you were informed of the disappearance of Mrs. Lindstrom's necklace, Miss Hunter, and you . . .'

'Discussed the matter with Mr. Dixie,' Miss Hunter carried on smoothly. 'He informed me that he had seen Miss Roubin leaving Mrs. Lindstrom's bedroom earlier that day. I knew that Mrs. Lindstrom was visiting her friends on the yacht *Nimrod.*' For a moment her eyes flickered towards Mr. Harvey, but he was not looking at her, he was drawing something on his blotter, his face grave. 'It also happened,' Miss Hunter went on dispassionately, 'that I had just been having a few words with the doctor. He had complained to me about the number of people who call him in for imaginary ailments. He was particularly annoyed with Miss Roubin, who had, he said, pestered him that afternoon, insisting that the child, Deborah, was ill, and asking for a sedative for the child so that she could go to bed.' Miss Hunter smiled, her eyes suddenly bright. 'It struck me that this could be a contrived story. I discussed it with Mr. Dixie and we decided we would search Miss Roubin's room. I wanted to avoid a scandal and I thought that the sooner we found and returned the necklace the better. We found the necklace, hidden in her suitcase.'

No one spoke for a moment. Lauren looked down at the hankie she was twisting in her hands. She was conscious that her cheeks were hot. Did she look guilty? How convincing Miss Hunter made it sound. Lauren glanced quickly at Roland Harvey. He was leaning on the desk, his eyes gravely interested, as he waited for Miss Hunter to continue.

Miss Hunter drew a deep breath, straightening herself still more, and leaned forward. 'Frankly, Mr. Harvey, we're wasting valuable time. I see no call to conduct an inquiry. The girl convicted herself when she admitted to fabricating that story.'

'It was no fabrication,' Lauren said quickly. 'Deborah was really—'

Roland Harvey interrupted, frowning a little. 'Shall we say that you thought Deborah was ill? Now, Miss Roubin, how can you account for the fact that the necklace was found in your suitcase?'

She put out her hands unconsciously. 'I can't. I had no idea that Mrs. Lindstrom's necklace had been stolen until I went to my room and saw it there. You were with me, Mr. Harvey,' she said.

'And that's the first time you saw the necklace yesterday?'

Lauren stared at him unhappily. Should she lie? His blue-grey eyes met hers steadily and she said: 'No. I had seen the necklace before.'

He leaned forward and his voice was quiet. 'Where?' he demanded.

Lauren stared down at her twisted, tormented hankie. 'I'd—I'd rather not say.' How could she tell the truth without implicating Natalie?

'You see!' Miss Hunter's voice was triumphant. 'Every time she opens her mouth, she convicts herself.'

'One moment, please, Miss Hunter,' Roland Harvey said sternly. 'Mr. Natal,' he turned to the silent Nick, 'do I understand that you stopped Miss Roubin this morning when she was on her way to the airstrip? She was planning to return to England and you knew nothing about it?'

Miss Hunter's face was excited. 'She was

running away?' she said eagerly. Her two hands came together with a sharp clap. 'What more do you want, Mr. Harvey? Only a guilty person would run away.'

'Mr. Harvey, I was not running away. You know why I was going, and so does Miss Hunter.' Lauren clenched her hands tightly, trying to steady her voice. 'This morning Miss Hunter came to my room and told me that you said I was to leave the island at once. I was to catch the nine o'clock plane, Miss Hunter said, there would be a car waiting for me at the door. She said that you had said I was to speak to no one in the hotel . . . guests or staff. She said it was your orders.'

Roland Harvey frowned as he looked at her. 'You believed that story? Surely you're not going to tell me that you believed I would condemn any person unheard? I thought you knew me better than that.'

Bewildered, Lauren looked at his grave face. 'Then . . . then Miss Hunter was lying?'

Miss Hunter was on her feet. She aimed an accusing finger at Lauren. 'You're the one who is lying. I've never heard such nonsense in my life. As if Mr. Harvey would behave like that! He is a just man. The whole story is a fantastic lie. I did not give her any such message. I haven't see her before today until now.' Her voice had grown shrill. Now she turned to Roland Harvey, holding out her hands, her voice quiet and controlled again. 'Mr. Harvey,

I worked for your uncle for many years and he trusted me implicitly. I thought I had earned your trust, too. You must believe me, and not this—this—' She almost choked over the word she did not say. 'How can I work for you—or you employ me—if you have no trust in me? This girl is a liar, and not a very good one at that.'

Lauren said, her voice desperate: 'I did not steal that necklace.'

She looked at Roland Harvey's grave face, saw the sadness in his eyes, the sternness of his mouth, and knew that he did not believe her.

## CHAPTER TWELVE

The door opened suddenly and Mrs. Lindstrom stood in the doorway, looking puzzled and annoyed. 'You want to see me, Roland?' she said coldly. How beautiful she looks, Lauren thought unhappily, as the tall, slim, poised woman wearing a green sheath frock entered the room. 'Is it really necessary to go on with this ugliness?' Mrs. Lindstrom asked. 'I've got my necklace and you've got the thief.'

Roland Harvey, who had risen immediately, now went to her side and led her to a chair. 'We have not found the thief yet,' he said quietly. 'Guilt has to be proved. Be patient with me and I won't keep you long.'

She shrugged, her mouth sulky, but she sat down. Roland Harvey looked at Nick and gave an almost imperceptible nod. Nick hurriedly left the room, and Lauren wondered where he had gone, as Roland Harvey returned to the desk. Meanwhile Miss Hunter, now she was no longer the centre of attraction, had sat down.

It all seemed completely unreal to Lauren. It was as if she was watching a film or a scene out of a play. Surely this was not happening to her?

She was even more surprised when Natalie came into the room, Nick holding her arm. Natalie looked pale and unhappy and she gave Lauren a quick look before she sat down as Mr. Harvey told her to. Nick perched on the arm of her chair, one hand on her shoulder.

Roland Harvey smiled at her. 'Mrs. Natal, I understand you can help us in this matter?'

Natalie bent her head, carefully folding pleats in her blue silk frock. Her voice was very quiet. 'Yes, Mr. Harvey, I found the necklace.' She looked up suddenly. 'But I didn't steal it. I didn't steal it. I—I found it . . . in the conservatory.' She looked round the room at every face, her expression defiant, almost as if she expected someone would contradict her.

'Natalie,' Nick said quietly, 'no one is—or will—accuse you of stealing the necklace. Just tell your story.'

Natalie seemed to huddle in the chair, her

voice unhappy.

'I was reading in the conservatory and I heard a child's voice. I—I recognized Deborah's. I looked round and saw her playing with her doll.'

'Alone?' Mrs. Lindstrom asked sharply.

Natalie nodded. 'I couldn't see what she was doing, but it looked as if she was putting something round the doll's neck. Then I heard her say distinctly—you know the way she can't say her "r's' because of her missing teeth?— well, she said: "You'll be pwetty one day. All little girls are pwetty, my fwiend says so, but I'll make you pwetty now."' Natalie's laugh was apologetic. 'I'm not awfully fond of children and I never know what to talk to them about, so I just sat quietly and went on reading and I forgot all about her. It was later when I got up to go that I saw she had gone and that her doll was there, and round its neck was a topaz necklace.'

Lauren let out her breath slowly and relaxed. So that was how Natalie got the necklace!

'Deborah must have taken the necklace from my jewel box,' Mrs. Lindstrom said, her voice hard and angry.

'Don't you keep it locked?' Roland Harvey asked. Mrs. Lindstrom looked at him. 'Of course I do, but but I was in a hurry yesterday morning when I went out, and I must have forgotten.'

203

Natalie went on, her voice sounding louder as if she was gathering confidence, 'I recognized it immediately. I also knew that Mrs. Lindstrom had gone to the yacht for the day, and I thought the simplest thing to do was to keep it and return it to her myself. I was admiring the necklace when Lauren came in . . .'

'So that was where you saw the necklace yesterday, Miss Roubin?'

Lauren looked at Roland Harvey and nodded. 'Yes.'

She felt ashamed of herself. How could she ever have thought Natalie would steal the necklace and put it in her room? Yet someone had. Who?

Natalie went on: 'Actually, I rather wondered why she didn't mention them and ask me where I got the beautiful stones. Then Nick came in and he said they must be handed in at once. He said if I wasn't careful I could be accused of having stolen them. I'm afraid I lost my temper and gave them to him . . .' She leaned back in her chair and looked at Nick.

Nick took over. 'I was worried, quite frankly. I was afraid that if we were found with them, the truth might be distorted and we'd find ourselves in big trouble. I put the necklace in a box, tied it up and sealed the knots. I gave it to the page, Petrus, to take to the reception desk. I addressed it to Miss Hunter, for I knew all lost articles had to be handed in to her.' He stretched his long legs, leaning against the back of the chair, his hand still on his wife's shoulder. 'I watched the page hand the packet to Rod Cay who was on duty at the desk, and I saw him give the packet to Miss Hunter.'

Miss Hunter seemed to come to life as she jumped to her feet. 'That's a lie! He's in league with that girl. I took no package from Cay.'

Nick stood up, his smile mocking. 'Shall we call Mr. Cay, sir?' he suggested.

Roland Harvey tapped his fingers on the desk and looked at the angry woman and then at Nick. 'That's not necessary, thank you,' he said coldly. 'I've already spoken to Cay.'

Miss Hunter's face went very white and she seemed to collapse in her chair and sat, tense and pale, staring at him.

'Miss Hunter,' Roland went on quietly, 'I have a few questions to ask you, and then I think we may consider the inquiry closed. First, who made the booking for Miss Roubin to fly on the plane to London this morning? Who ordered the car to be waiting for her? Lastly, who informed you of the theft of Mrs. Lindstrom's necklace?'

Miss Hunter did not answer. She stared at him, her throat jerking convulsively. Mr. Harvey turned to Mrs. Lindstrom.

'When did you first discover your necklace was missing? Could you give me the exact time?'

Mrs. Lindstrom answered immediately. 'Of course I can. It was just after ten o'clock last night. I didn't change my jewellery when I came back from—from the yacht, as I was late. I was tired during the evening, so I went up to my room at about ten o'clock. It was when I was putting away my earrings that I noticed that the necklace was not there. I would say about ten minutes past ten. I came straight down to tell you and—'

Roland Harvey smiled. 'Thank you, Leila, that was all I needed to know.' He turned to Miss Hunter, and Lauren shivered with unexpected sympathy for her as he said: 'So it would seem, Miss Hunter, that you are the only person, apart from Mr. and Mrs. Natal, who was aware that the necklace was not in Mrs. Lindstrom's jewel case. This can only be because—in the right pursuance of your duties—you opened the package and found the necklace. We can only presume that, for reasons of your own, you hid the necklace in Miss Roubin's suitcase, involved Mr. Dixie very cleverly, and so discovered the necklace.'

'Why should I do a thing like that?' Miss Hunter's voice was thick and guttural, as if she could hardly speak. Her face was scarlet, her hands were gripping the arms of her chair. 'It's all lies . . . lies . . . lies!' Her voice rose shrilly to a scream.

'Unfortunately, it isn't,' Roland Harvey said quietly, standing up. 'I don't think I need keep any of you here any longer. This is a matter between Miss Hunter and myself.'

He opened the door, standing by it silently, as they filed out, Mrs. Lindstrom first, Nick and Natalie together. Lauren looked at the woman in the chair, who had crumpled into a heap and hidden her face in her hands.

At the door, Lauren paused, glancing up into Roland Harvey's stern face. 'Why should she do a thing like that to me?' she asked softly. She shivered a little at the thought of what might have happened had Roland Harvey been content to take Miss Hunter's word—had there been no Nick to catch her on the way to the airstrip, to face Mr. Harvey.

Roland Harvey put his hand under her elbow and hurried her out of the room. 'We'll talk later,' he said quietly, and then closed the door between them.

The others had vanished, and Lauren, feeling absurdly alone and still a little sick with shock, hurried to her room. There she stood for a while, gazing out of the wide open windows at the beautiful scene. So much beauty and yet so much ugliness . . . how could Miss Hunter have hated her so much? Why?

Lauren realized suddenly that it was time for the children's class and she hurried to get ready for it. It would stop her thinking . . .

Deborah was not at the class, and Lauren worried a little. How was the child? Had she awakened without any memory of her fright?

How terrified she must have been of her mother's anger to have collapsed like that into a tearful, shocked child.

Later, sitting on the sands under their palm tree, Lauren worried still more. Something made her turn her head and she saw, walking across the sands towards her with his long easy stride, Roland Harvey. He looked thoughtful, his mouth was stern, and his eyes hidden by his dark glasses. He still wore his light tropical suit, so evidently he had no intention of relaxing and swimming with them.

'I knew I'd find you here,' he said, and sat down on the hot sand by her side. 'Isn't Deborah with you?'

Lauren turned to him. 'I'm worried about her. I hope she is all right. She was very frightened and upset yesterday. She didn't come to the dancing class, and she hates missing that.' Impulsively Lauren went on: 'I do hope her mother won't punish her.'

He frowned, and she knew that she had said the wrong thing.

'Leila Lindstrom wouldn't punish the child,' he said rebukingly. 'After all, Deborah had no idea that the necklace was so valuable. It's just like the bead necklaces she makes for her doll.' He frowned again. 'Poor little brat. She said nothing to you about it when she was crying?'

'Nothing. She couldn't talk properly. She was quite hysterical, sobbing bitterly.' She leaned down and traced a pattern in the sand with her finger, not wanting to look at him. How very quickly he had leaped to Mrs. Lindstrom's defence.

'Lauren,' he said gravely, 'how can I apologize to you for the unpleasantness Miss Hunter caused?'

She wished he would take off his dark glasses so that she could see the colour of his eyes. 'She confessed?' she asked.

Roland Harvey shrugged. 'What else could she do? She became hysterical and almost violent, I had to send for the doctor and he gave her an injection.'

Neither spoke for a moment, and then he sighed: 'How can a woman of her ethics and intelligence behave like that?'

'I can't think why she hates me so much,' Lauren said sadly. 'I don't know what I've ever done to—'

Roland Harvey smiled. 'Look in your mirror and you'll see the answer, Lauren. You have youth, beauty, personality—everything on your side. She must be in her late forties, is single, frustrated. What I can't get over is how you could possibly believe that I would behave like that.' His voice sounded vexed and hurt. 'You must have known I wouldn't be unjust— packing you off like a—a criminal, forbidding you to speak to anyone.' He sounded shocked. 'Surely you trusted me?'

Lauren looked at him. 'You believed I was a

thief,' she said.

He leant forward and took off her sunglasses and stared into her eyes. 'I never believed it for a second,' he said quietly.

'Yes, you did. Last night.' Suddenly, horrifyingly, her voice was trembling. 'You looked at me—and I knew.' She looked away from him, struggling for control. 'You—you said we would continue—continue the next day, and . . .'

'Look at me, Lauren,' he said sternly, and stared down into her tear-filled eyes. 'I've already told you that last night you were emotionally upset. I knew you would hate crying in front of Mr. Dixie or Miss Hunter.' He smiled suddenly, a singularly sweet smile. 'You know how you always get tearful if I speak too kindly to you . . . I didn't dare say anything lest I upset you. I thought you would know that I trust you.'

She found herself smiling through her tears. 'I don't know why I cry so easily these days,' she admitted. 'I never used to.' She looked at him shyly. 'You didn't doubt me for one moment?'

'Of course not,' he said, almost impatiently. 'I'm a good judge of character.' He paused, smiling ruefully, rubbing his hand thoughtfully over his chin. Behind him she could see the glorious vista of the white sands and the blue sea. Voices and laughter drifted through the air. 'I wonder if I am,' he went on thoughtfully.

'I'll confess that I never liked Nick. I thought he was smooth, facile. Today I've changed my mind. He is a good man. Take Miss Hunter—I would have staked my oath that she was to be trusted completely. I know my uncle thought a great deal of her. Yet now—to behave like this! It beats me,' he said wearily.

The slang was so out of keeping with his normal conversation that Lauren looked at him and saw that he meant it. She longed to comfort him. 'Perhaps she's like you said Natalie was,' Lauren said nervously. 'Mixed-up, jealous. I heard that she always thought your uncle would marry her.'

Roland Harvey looked startled. He took off his sunglasses and began to rub them with his handkerchief. 'I had no idea of that. He wasn't a marrying man. He was a perfectly happy old bachelor. But it's odd you should say that, for his last few letters to me gave me the impression that he was worried about something. I thought it might be the hotel.' He frowned. 'Maybe she'll be happier now. Did I tell you I was going to sell the hotel? Who do you think made me the best offer for it?'

'I don't know,' Lauren admitted. She was always surprised and a little proud when Roland Harvey discussed his affairs with her.

He smiled. 'You'd never guess. I had a surprise. Miss Hunter, of all people. It seems it has been her ambition to own the Island Hotel, but she must be a very shrewd business woman to have invested her earnings so well. After all, although she earns a good salary, it's not all that large.'

'I suppose when you add the percentage of all salaries that she takes, it could add up to quite a bit. After all, you have a very big staff,' Lauren said thoughtfully, trying to sound intelligent.

Roland Harvey swung round to stare at her. 'What did you say?' he demanded. He leant towards her and his hand gripped her arm. 'Say that again. A percentage of all salaries?'

Startled and, as usual, nervous because of his abrupt change of moods, she told him what Nick had told her. 'Rene—in charge of linen on my floor—told me the same. She says that if they don't pay Miss Hunter the percentage she sacks them.' Lauren's eyes were wide with dismay. It was so easy to vex this man. Would he accuse her of snooping?

'I knew nothing of this,' he said sternly. 'I'm sure my uncle didn't, either. He would never have condoned it. Why wasn't I told?'

'No one can talk to you,' Lauren pointed out timidly. 'As you know, Miss Hunter handles all the staff and . . . and has the power to dismiss them as well as to engage them.'

Roland Harvey ran his hand through his hair so that it looked quite ruffled. 'I don't understand,' he said wearily. 'What must a man do to win the confidence of his staff?' He stared at Lauren. 'I did my best. I interviewed them all in turn, since you've been here, and not one of them told me of this, or complained about Miss Hunter.'

'They were scared,' Lauren said. 'You see, they know you leave everything to her. They thought if they told you, you would either not believe them, or ask Miss Hunter, and she would deny it. Or you would tell Miss Hunter which of the staff were dissatisfied, and very soon they would get the sack. As good jobs like these aren't easy to find, Rene said they decided to keep their mouths shut and . . . and . . .' Her words died away beneath the fury of his gaze.

'Then why didn't you tell me?' he demanded.

'You trusted Miss Hunter. You would have believed her and she would have said I lied. She would have said I was trying to make trouble, that I didn't know what I was talking about, and . . .'

He sighed and shook his head. 'I still can't believe it.'

'You see?' Lauren said indignantly. 'Just what I said. You don't believe me. You always think I'm lying.'

He turned suddenly and caught her by her shoulders, pulling her towards him, gazing down into her eyes. 'I know you're not lying,' he said roughly. As he looked at her, his expression changed, and as abruptly as he had seized her, so he released her. He stood up

213

with one of his graceful quick movements. Now his voice was formal. 'You must excuse me, I have work to do.'

She watched him walk away and then made herself relax, thinking again and again what a strange man he was. How quickly he changed. She closed her eyes and shivered as she thought that if Nick had not seen her that morning and stopped her, by now she would be in London, dreary fog-ridden London, facing Miss Cartwright's wrath, her parents' surprise and dismay. How very close to disaster she had been. Roland Harvey would have seen it—as Miss Hunter planned—as an admission of guilt; Nick would never have forgiven her. How could she have believed Miss Hunter? Yet at the time she had been so confused and unhappy, and Miss Hunter had seemed so convincing.

That afternoon at practice, Lauren saw Roland Harvey standing in the doorway. The tall, broad-shouldered man seemed to fill the doorway as he stood, immaculate in a light tropical suit, his arms folded, his face grave.

They were practising an Apache dance, and Lauren felt nervous as she kept catching glimpses of the brooding figure in the doorway, but at last Nick declared himself satisfied and the orchestra folded their music and put away their instruments, just as Roland walked across the floor towards them.

'Have you seen Deborah?' he asked.

Lauren hesitated. She must choose her words carefully, for she had angered him that morning by her suggestion that Mrs. Lindstrom might punish the child.

'No,' she said. 'I expect she's gone with her mother.'

Roland frowned. 'I doubt it very much,' he said dryly. 'She was spending the day on the *Nimrod* with the Brandons, who are not fond of children.' He turned away. 'She must be all right.'

Lauren stared after him unhappily. She wished she could feel as confident. She remembered Deborah's tear-stained, scared little face and her heart seemed to turn over with pain.

At the same moment someone came hurrying through the door. Tall, slim, lovely in her lime green silk suit, Mrs. Lindstrom's calm had vanished as she almost ran to Lauren, grabbing her arm.

'Where is she? You have no right . . .' she said angrily.

'Leila, what's wrong?' Roland Harvey said as he hurried to her side.

Mrs. Lindstrom's face seemed to crumple. 'It's all my fault, Roland. I was so angry with Deborah . . .' She looked round her wildly. 'The child must be somewhere.' She turned back to him, her face working painfully, her hands outstretched. 'Roland, Deborah's father was like that. He would play practical jokes that weren't funny. He would hide my jewels or my money and then scold me for being careless, and much, much later he would return them to me and laugh. I felt I couldn't bear it if Deborah had inherited the habit. She was so strange this morning when I scolded her . . . anyhow I'm afraid I lost my temper and spanked her, hard, and then I told her she must stay in her room all day without anything to eat, as a punishment and—and I said if she ever stole anything again the police would put her in prison . . .'

Roland Harvey had his arm round Mrs. Lindstrom's shoulders, trying to comfort the distraught woman. Nick and Lauren looked at one another unhappily and longed to creep away quietly.

'And Deborah has gone from her room?' Roland Harvey said gently. 'What made you think Lauren had taken her?'

Mrs. Lindstrom moved away from him, mopping her eyes with a scrap of lace-trimmed linen. 'Because she's always with Miss Roubin,' she said sulkily.

'You've been out all day?' Roland Harvey's voice was still quiet and kind.

'Yes. You must remember the Brandons' cousin had asked me to go fishing with him today. I went to Deborah's room as soon as I got back. I had locked the door and left the key on the outside, and someone must have . . .' She glared accusingly at the silent Lauren.

'Released her,' Roland Harvey said. 'Perhaps they heard her crying.'

'Even if they did, they had no right to interfere. She is my child, and I have the right to discipline her . . .' Mrs. Lindstrom was regaining her composure, obviously stirring up her anger to hide her fear. 'But where is she, Roland?'

'We'll organize a search,' Roland Harvey said crisply. 'Go to bed, Leila, and I'll have your dinner sent up to you. Don't worry. The child must be somewhere near.' He smiled. 'At least we have no buses or trains for her to hide on! We'll soon find her. Whoever released her from the room will come forward as soon as they hear she is missing. Don't worry.'

'You think she's all right?' Mrs. Lindstrom said.

Roland Harvey nodded. 'I'm sure she is,' he said confidently. 'Now go along to your room and relax and stop worrying. Everything will be all right.'

Silently they watched the woman, whose shoulders drooped, walk away to the lift, and then Roland Harvey turned to his companions.

'Look in your room first, Lauren,' he said curtly. 'She might be hiding there.' He looked at Nick. 'Go and search the beach . . . oh, and look in the patch of flowering shrubs, the one Lauren usually uses. The child can't be far away.'

Lauren hurried to her room, but there was

217

no sign of Deborah. She felt sick with fear. Where could the child be? How could Mrs. Lindstrom have been so cruel? Why, the child was so young, too young to . . .

Yet Mr. Harvey had not seemed to be angry with Leila Lindstrom. His voice had been tender as he comforted her.

## CHAPTER THIRTEEN

Deborah was still missing five hours later. It had been a long, anxious time, and wearily Lauren changed out of the cream satin gown she had worn for the third dance, and pulled on a pink cotton frock. She washed her hair quickly, rubbing it with a towel, twisting the wet strands into a knot on her head, jabbing in a few hairpins. She did not stop to make up her face, but thrust her feet into sandals and hurried down to the hall.

Life in the hotel had continued as if nothing had happened, but of course everyone knew that the child was missing, and it affected everyone in some way. Lauren knew that Roland Harvey was out in the dark night, leading one of the search parties that were scouring the island. Every now and then the moon came out from behind the bank of thick clouds that had formed and then the whole scene became one of silvery magic. Mrs.

Lindstrom was reputed to be in bed, having been given a sedative by the doctor. Lauren also heard that boats with lights were exploring every lagoon and tiny creek on the island in case the child had slipped into the water by accident. Even the atmosphere in the ballroom had been affected. Nick and Lauren had danced with little spirit, and had not been surprised at the small applause they got. Both were impatient to be free to join in the search.

As Lauren stepped out of the lift in the large, luxurious entrance hall, Roland Harvey walked in. He looked tired and dusty, his white shorts and shirt stained.

'She must be somewhere,' he said desperately in answer to the question in her eyes. 'I need a drink. Let's pool our brains and see if we can't think of something.'

Over a long cool drink, they talked. Lauren thought hard.

'I would never expect her to come to me,' she said thoughtfully.

'She did yesterday,' he pointed out, slowly lighting a cigarette.

'She might . . .' Lauren began, and paused. 'I don't think so, this time. You see, she might have thought her mother meant the police would come soon and take her away. She would know I could only comfort her, that I had no influence with her mother.' Lauren's worried face suddenly brightened and her eyes were like stars. 'I've got it! Why, if I were a

219

child . . . when I was a child, I always ran to my father when my mother was cross. I knew he'd be on my side and he'd help me. Don't you see,' in her eagerness, she caught hold of his arm, 'that to Deborah, you are her father. She'd turn to you. She didn't mean to steal anything and she knew you'd make her mother understand.' He made no answer, so she went on: 'Can't you see that to Deborah you are already her father?'

'Already?' he echoed looking down at her eager young face so completely free from make-up, the wet hair, strained back carelessly.

Lauren was on her feet. 'Why didn't we think before? She wouldn't go to your office in case Miss Hunter went there.' Lauren stood, thinking hard, tapping her finger against her mouth. 'Where could she go where only you could find her? I've got it!' She beamed on the silent man. 'Why, your suite, of course.'

He caught up with her as she reached the lift. Worriedly, he looked at her excited face.

'Don't count on it. She's never been to my suite. I doubt if she knows where it is.'

Lauren tossed her head, laughing up at him. All at once she felt very gay. Deborah was all right! 'Of course she does. She's a very bright child and she knows everything about the hotel. After all, she thinks it will be hers one day.'

'Lauren,' he began, but the lift doors slid

open and Lauren was off down the passage, like a streak of lightning. She skidded to a halt outside his door, turned to look warningly at the tall good-looking man and laid her finger on her mouth.

Very, very gently, she turned the handle of the door and opened it. Together they crept inside.

The moon was shining through the wide open window, falling in its silvery beauty on the large, chintz-covered couch, and . . . Deborah, fast asleep, hugging a cushion tightly.

The tension left Lauren's body and she relaxed, sliding gratefully into a chair while she watched Roland's face as he bent over the sleeping child. She saw the tenderness in his glance, saw the gentle smile on his usually stern mouth. How he loved Deborah!

He straightened and looked at Lauren. 'Clever girl,' he said softly. 'Whatever made you think of this?'

'I was wondering what I would do if I was in trouble. I knew I'd run to you,' she said softly. Suddenly she realized what she had said, and was confused. 'I mean—I mean to her, you are her father, and I'd—I'd run to my father if I was in trouble.'

He studied her face gravely and then nodded.

'I understand,' he said, his voice suddenly flat.

221

He turned away and his manner changed. Gone was the warm friendliness, the intimacy they had shared in the search for Deborah. Once again he became the famous explorer, wealthy owner of this luxury hotel, the fabulous Roland Harvey. 'Thank you,' he said stiffly. 'I can handle this now.'

She was dismissed. Somehow she stood up and left the room, hurrying back to her own bedroom, flinging off her clothes in the dark, tumbling into bed, pressing her face against the cool linen of the pillow. She just could not understand him. She closed her eyes, picturing the scene when he carried Deborah back to her mother—what a beautiful little group they would make.

She could not bear to think of it. She must go to sleep. She closed her eyes tightly, trying to imagine a stile with sheep jumping over it . . . Only she couldn't see any sheep, only Roland Harvey's rugged handsome face, his strange blue-grey eyes, his smile.

She overslept next morning and dressed hastily. Claudia brought her breakfast and seemed to want to talk, but Lauren was in no mood for gossip so she did not encourage her. Lauren was filled with the most terrible depression. All she longed to do was to pack her cases and go right away, away from the beautiful island where she had known both great happiness and much sorrow. Away—so that she could force herself to forget him, to accept the fact that he was going to marry Leila Lindstrom. She had flung on the first dress her hands found, a simple white sheath frock, and had brushed her hair back, tying it in a pony-tail. She made a face at her reflection in the mirror. How ridiculously young she looked. How she hated that young innocent look. How she hated her youth! Now if only she could be Mrs. Lindstrom's age—elegant, lovely, sophisticated. The type of woman to appeal to Roland Harvey.

In the reception hall, she was caught up in a buzz of excitement. Mr. Cay, behind his desk, came hurrying to meet her.

'Such goings on, miss!' he said eagerly. He was a nice-looking, friendly lad, Lauren thought. 'Miss Hunter has been packed off for some reason or other. No one seems to know. She went on the nine o'clock plane—and what do you think, miss, Mr. Harvey is going to turn the hotel into a limited company and we can all get shares in it!' His eyes were bright, his voice excited. 'It seems he didn't know anything about Miss Hunter getting a slice of our wages, and he's mad about it. Says he's going to make it up to us by giving us shares in the hotel. Oh, boy, who knows, one day I might be a millionaire!' He saw someone approaching his desk and nipped back to his place very sharply.

Lauren stood very still. Roland hadn't lost much time. It was a wonderful idea. How

223

much more interest and pride in the hotel the staff would take if they felt it belonged to them. Quite suddenly Lauren knew the answer to her problems. She would go and ask Natalie if she felt strong enough to take over the dancing; she would say how much she wanted to leave the island. Miss Hunter had said Natalie was eager to, but then Miss Hunter had told a great many lies.

Suddenly happier, for she knew that she could not just wait for Roland Harvey to announce his engagement to Leila Lindstrom, Lauren turned to the lift again. She would go straight up and see Natalie.

'Miss Roubin . . . paging Miss Roubin!' Petrus was calling.

Lauren turned and saw the page boy, immaculate in starched white uniform, holding a note on a silver salver.

Lauren recognized the handwriting. Slowly she opened it.

'Please come to my office immediately.'

Carefully she folded it up and put it in her pocket. Lately she was always being asked to go to his office. What was it for this time? Reluctantly she went. She would tell him that she wanted to return to England, ask him if he would release her if Natalie was well enough to take her place.

Roland Harvey looked up from his desk. 'Please sit down. I won't be a moment,' he said formally.

She obeyed, looking round the large, luxuriously-furnished room sadly, with the feeling that this would be the last time she would ever see it.

The desk dominated the room—just as the man dominated every place he went. She looked at his neat dark red hair as he bent his head over the papers he was signing.

How wonderful it would have been had her dream come true. Imagine being that man's wife . . . leaning on him in trouble, comforting him when he was sad; being his partner in that most exciting of all partnerships, marriage. Of course she would suffer when he went off on one of his expeditions, but she would learn to hide her unhappiness, just as her mother had done. The happiness she would have had when he was with her would have been reward enough.

Roland Harvey suddenly stood up and came to sit on the couch by her side. She was quite unprepared for the remark he shot at her:

'Tell me about this man you love.'

'The man I love?' she echoed.

'Yes, yes,' he said impatiently. 'The man you were telling me about. This man you think you're in love with. I thought it was Nick, but you said it wasn't. Your parents said nothing to me about it. Do they know?'

She stared at him. 'No,' she said.

He frowned. 'Would they approve if they did know?'

This, at least, she could answer truthfully. 'Oh, yes, they certainly would,' she said warmly, her eyes bright. 'They couldn't help it. He's . . . he's . . .'

'Wonderful?' Roland supplied the word dryly.

'Oh, yes, he is,' she could still say truthfully. How thrilled her parents would be if Roland Harvey was their son-in-law.

'I see.' His hands were clasped loosely between his knees and he looked down at them as he went on. 'You must miss him. I expect you'll be getting married soon. Long engagements are a mistake . . . Are you certain you love him?' he asked abruptly, turning to face her.

Startled, Lauren looked at him. Was he blind? Surely her love for him showed in her eyes, sounded in her voice? She looked away from him quickly. 'Yes, I am certain,' she said.

He stood up, began to walk about the room. 'I think it would be as well for you to return to England at once,' he said curtly, almost flinging the words at her. 'Natalie and her husband both seem to think she could cope with simple dances now, so that would release you.' His voice was authoritative, as if everything had been arranged.

Lauren shrank back in the corner of the couch. He was sending her away. Somehow it seemed a thousand times worse than when she had planned to leave herself. He wanted to get rid of her. Why? What had she done?

He went and stood by the window, talking over his shoulder, not looking at her. 'Then that's settled. Discuss it with Nick and let me know when you want to go. I hope you'll be very happy.'

Very slowly, feeling as if something had died inside her, Lauren stood up and walked to the door. She stared at the straight implacable back of the tall man. 'Thank you, Mr. Harvey,' she said quietly. Her throat felt tight. Somehow she found strength enough to say politely: 'I hope you will be very happy, Mr. Harvey—you and Mrs. Lindstrom.'

He swung round. 'Now what exactly do you mean by that?' he asked, striding across the room. 'You're always linking my name with that woman's.' Lauren's hand was on the door knob.

'Aren't you going to marry her?' she asked. He towered above her. 'Who told you that?'

Her mouth was dry. 'Deborah said you were going to be her new daddy.'

He seemed to relax. 'Wishful thinking. She needs a father badly. Well, she's getting one, but I'm afraid he dislikes children. Mrs. Lindstrom is going to marry the Brandons' cousin, Felix Nottar.'

Lauren stared at him. 'You're not going to marry her,' she said very slowly, feeling the knowledge seep through her veins.

He clasped his hands behind his back and

stared down at her.

'Of course I'm not,' he said curtly. 'Never any question of it. Felix is extremely handsome and very wealthy.'

Such a wave of happiness flooded her that she could hardly speak. Then she realized what this must mean to him.

He frowned impatiently. 'Nothing to be sorry about.' Lauren hesitated. 'I thought . . . you see, you were always together, and . . .'

'Didn't it strike you that I was fond of Deborah and sorry for her? The only way I could help her was by being friendly with her mother.' He frowned. 'I was never in love with her.'

Lauren drew a long deep breath. Impulsively, she clasped her hands, staring at him. 'Oh, how I wish I'd known,' she said softly and from her heart. And then she realized what she had said, and her hand flew to her mouth in dismay.

But Roland Harvey had not noticed. He had gone to stand by his desk, spinning a heavy silver ash tray round and round.

'We have discovered,' he said stiffly, 'that it was your friend Rene who let Deborah out of her bedroom. She heard her crying. She knew nothing of the child's disappearance, for she was taken ill that afternoon with mild food poisoning and no one thought to tell her. I have suggested to Deborah's mother that the child would be happier at a good boarding

228

school. Her mother is going to China for her honeymoon, and later they plan to cruise throughout the world, and they don't want a child along.' He paused, giving the ash tray a final spin before turning to look at Lauren. 'I hope that perhaps, in the future, Leila might let me adopt Deborah.'

'That would be wonderful,' Lauren said eagerly. 'Deborah loves you so, and she badly needs to be loved.'

'Don't we all?' Roland Harvey said quietly, so quietly that Lauren wondered if she had heard him aright.

'I beg your pardon. What did you say?' she asked.

His face was grave. 'I said—don't we all want to be loved? How fortunate you are, Lauren, to love a man who loves you.'

She stared at him and misery filled her. 'I wish he did . . . but he d—doesn't . . .' she whispered.

Suddenly Roland was by her side. 'How do you know?' he asked her. His hands were on her shoulders as he forced her to look up at him. 'Lauren,' he said gently, 'is it possible that it's true—what Nick told me? Miss Hunter said . . . but I didn't believe her. Lauren,' his voice was suddenly stern, 'tell me the name of the man you love.'

She looked into his fascinatingly strange eyes and saw her face reflected in them. She saw other things, too. She saw wonder,

229

happiness, tenderness, love. 'Can't you guess?' she said softly. 'The name is Roland Harvey.'

'Darling . . . darling!' he murmured, and his arms closed round her and his mouth came down hard on hers.

She clung to him. She felt she could not hold him close enough. Was this wonderful thing really happening to her?

'I can't believe it,' she kept saying.

He lifted her up in his arms and carried her to the couch, sitting down, still holding her close in his arms, gazing at her radiant face as if he had never seen her before.

'I can't believe it either,' he said. 'This wonderful thing happening to me!'

She smiled at him. 'That's just how I feel.'

They stared at one another, each trying to realize that it was true.

'But what can you see in me?' he asked. 'A bachelor, selfish, set in my ways, fifteen years older than you, bad-tempered, while you are a lovely young girl, with the world at your feet.'

Lauren laughed softly and laid her cheek against his.

'You're too modest. I think you're the most wonderful man in the whole world. Are you sure you love me?'

'Quite sure,' he told her. He whispered the most beautiful words in the English language against her soft mouth: 'I love you, my darling.'

Now she had the right to stroke his dark red

hair, to trace the line of his jaw, to lay her cheek against his, to kiss his tender mouth shyly. 'I can't believe it,' she whispered again.

He kissed her, gently, then with a deep intensity that made her fling her arms round his neck and give him her ardent young mouth. At last he let her go and they stared at one another, both a little shaken.

'It is true,' Roland said unsteadily.

'It is true.' She smiled at him and then thought of something. 'You were going to send me away.'

He smiled. 'I had to know the truth, Lauren, the truth about the man you loved. I wanted to believe Nick when he told me that no man in the world existed for you but me.' He laughed again. 'I had to know. And . . . and I had to know if he was wrong and you loved someone else. I couldn't bear it any longer. Wasn't I a fool?' he said softly.

'I was a fool, too,' she confessed. 'I was on my way to ask Natalie if she could take over. I was going to ask you to let me go back to England. I felt I couldn't bear it if I had to watch you marrying someone else.' She kissed the corner of his mouth very lightly. 'I love you so, darling, darling. This is like a dream come true.'

'Paradise Island is a place where dreams come true,' he said. 'All my life I've been searching for something, and I didn't know what it was. And then I met you—and I knew.'

'I knew in London, at that lecture, when you first walked on to that platform,' she told him delightedly.

He smiled. 'And I was so jealous of this man you said you loved. I knew you belonged to another man, so I had no right . . .'

'When Deborah told me you were going to be her new daddy, I thought my heart would break,' Lauren confessed.

They smiled at one another. So much to talk about, so much to discover, and all the time in the world in which to do it.

'What will you do with the hotel?' she asked.

He told her. It was just as Mr. Cay had said. It would be a company, giving the employees the chance to buy shares, to be given shares as a bonus. 'I don't think I shall want to go roaming any more,' Roland told her. 'Now I've got someone to make staying at home worthwhile.'

'We could give special terms to honeymoon couples,' Lauren said eagerly after she had thanked him with a kiss.

'How about asking your family over? Would you like that?' he wondered.

She hugged him. 'Darling, that's a wonderful idea. They were terribly impressed by you.' She stroked his hair tenderly. Suddenly she was worried. 'Oh dear, I do hope I make you a good wife. I'm afraid I'm not elegant or sophisticated like Mrs. Lindstrom.'

'Thanks be!' he said fervently. 'I fell in love with you because you were so refreshingly young and unspoiled. If you were like Leila Lindstrom, I'd start running.' He laughed down at her.

She put her arms round his neck, resting her cheek against his.

'If you ran, I'd chase you,' she said softly. 'And I'd catch you!' She laughed happily. 'Make up your mind to it, darling dearest, I'll never . . . ever . . . let you go.'

'You'll never be able to,' he promised. 'I'll never . . . ever . . . want to go,' he added, and held her very close as he sealed the promise with a kiss.